I0563741

THE ACCEPTANCE

BERNADETTE MARIE

5 PRINCE PUBLISHING

ISBN DIGITAL: 978-1-63112-036-7

ISBN PRINT: 978-1-63112-037-4

The Acceptance, Bernadette Marie

Copyright Bernadette Marie 2014

Published by 5 Prince Publishing

4th version/printing 2021

12-8

For Stan,
You make accepting the things I can't change easier
by just being by my side...always.

ACKNOWLEDGMENTS

For Stan who validates me everyday by supporting me, encouraging me, respecting my time working at home, and never ever complaining about domestic things that are overlooked.

For my Fab 5 who accept me with every flaw I have, and who teach me every day, something new to better myself.

For Mom, Dad, and Anni who have always accepted me—me who piles things everywhere, loses things always, talks non-stop, and dreams excessively BIG!

For Connie and Clare who accept my horrible organization skills with humor and love, and always continue to keep me on track!

For Sara and June who accept manuscripts written late at night, with my eyes closed, and diligently make them look nice.

For Jo, who had no choices when she became my suite-mate in college, who accepted the challenges set before her as a woman who faced the world without eyesight. She taught me more than I ever knew. You can see quite a bit without physically seeing anything.

ALSO BY BERNADETTE MARIE

Date for Hire

THE DEVEREAUX FAMILY SERIES

Kennedy Devereaux

Chase Devereaux

Max Devereaux

Paige Devereaux

FUNERALS AND WEDDINGS SERIES

Something Lost

Something Discovered

Something Found

Something Forbidden

Something New

THE ACCEPTANCE

CHAPTER 1

There was something about an airport. People were coming and going. Some were heading out for adventure, and some were heading home—just like Tyler Benson.

Nashville would always be home. He'd taken nearly three years to see the world and think his life through. He wasn't sure he had a better grasp on it yet, but he knew one thing—he missed his family.

Why had he let his mother's choices affect him so much? Things must have been pretty bad for her if she gave up a child and never spoke of it again.

The man in him understood. His mother was protecting Tyler and his brother from what had happened to her when she'd fallen in love with an abusive man who tried to kill her. But the boy in Tyler was still hurt.

Heading back wouldn't fix everything. He assumed there'd be a lot of late night talks over the kitchen table as there had been when he was a teenager. His father already had offered him a good job in the construction firm which had been in the family for generations. And—he needed to finally get to really know his sister.

Darcy had been as shocked as Tyler when she'd learned who her mother was. After all, she'd fallen in love with Tyler's cousin —that had to have been a little odd once they all knew the truth. But the Keller family was eclectic. It was made up of many adopted children, but they were still one big family.

Tyler's cousin Ed and his sister Darcy had been married over a year now. Their wedding had been the only time Tyler had been home in three years. Now it was time to face his parents and ask for some forgiveness, which he was sure they'd give him. Everyone understood his need to find himself.

The voice over the speaker called for his flight from New York to Nashville. It was time to board the plane. He stood and moved toward the line as a woman ran right into him.

"I'm so sorry," she said quickly.

"It's no problem." He looked down and noticed she'd dropped her scarf. "You dropped this." He bent down to pick it up and hand it to her.

The woman only held out her hand, but didn't reach for it. Tyler placed it in her open hand.

"Oh, thank you. I lose more things." She gave a casual laugh. It was then he noticed the white cane in her other hand.

"Do you need an arm to get on the plane?" Tyler asked, realizing she was blind.

The woman smiled at him, though her eyes were shielded behind big sunglasses. "Are you a nice man or do you feel sorry for me?"

That was quite a question, he thought. "Well, I'd like to think it was because I was raised right."

"You're from the South." She chewed her bottom lip in thought. "Tennessee?"

"Yes. Born and raised in Nashville."

She leaned in closer to him. "I guessed from your accent and since we're getting on a flight bound that way."

He couldn't help but chuckle. "Offer still holds."

"What's your name?"

"I'm Tyler. Tyler Benson."

"Courtney Field. And, Mr. Benson, I'd love to have you guide me if you don't mind."

"It would be my pleasure."

Tyler let her take his arm, though she didn't interlock elbows, instead she held the back of his arm just above his elbow.

When they approached the door, Courtney held out her ticket, the woman scanned it, and placed the stub back in her hand. She then did the same for Tyler.

Once checked in, they walked down the jet bridge.

"Do you travel a lot, Mr. Benson?"

"It's Tyler, and I've been doing my fair share the past few years. How about you?"

"I've been seeing the world, though not intentionally. So yes, I travel quite a bit. But this is a special trip back home."

Tyler desperately wanted to ask her why she said she'd been seeing the world. Could she see? Was it just a figure of speech?

"Hello, Ms. Field." The flight attendant greeted her as they walked on board.

"Celia." Courtney smiled, having obviously recognized the woman's voice. "I didn't expect you on this flight."

"I'm state side now." Celia took Courtney's hand, which still held her cane, and patted it. "I've heard we have your brother on board," she said softly.

Courtney nodded. "Finally."

"Your family has been in my thoughts for a long time."

"Thank you," Courtney said. "Oh, Celia, this is Tyler. My arm candy for the walk down the jet way."

Celia looked at Tyler and back at Courtney. "I thought you had an escort."

"It's always good to make a new friend. How does he look?"

Celia scanned another look over Tyler. "You did good."

Tyler forced a smile. "Thank you?"

Celia laughed. "Courtney, can I help you find your seat?"

"If you don't mind, I'll use my arm candy."

Tyler looked at her ticket. "You're in 3A."

"Yep, that sounds right. Where are you?"

"I'm in 4F."

"You like the window too?"

"Luck of the draw really."

Courtney stopped and turned back to Celia. "Can you arrange my escort to trade to 4F?"

The smile on Celia's face and the look she casually gave to Tyler made him a little nervous. His good deed had warranted him a seat change?

"Do you mind sitting by me on the flight? I could use some good company," Courtney asked.

Tyler thought about the past three years and wondered if he could be good company. But, like he'd told her before, he'd been raised right. And if the woman wanted to sit by him, who was he to turn her down?

"If the other passenger doesn't mind changing, I'd be happy to switch."

"I still like the window. I hope that's okay," she said as she walked toward her seat.

Once they were seated, Courtney turned to him. "Thank you for picking up my scarf."

"You're welcome."

"Thanks for keeping me company. This trip home is a hard one and it'll be nice to have a handsome man to talk to."

Tyler wondered what made her trip so hard, besides the obvious hindrance of not being able to see the world around her.

"How do you know I'm so handsome? Celia might have been lying to you."

She smiled. "Oh, I can tell you're handsome. And you're not married. I would guess you're in your mid to late twenties. You were well educated. You're about six-two. And you have blue eyes."

He knew that staring at her with his eyes wide open wasn't going to make her aware of how stunned he was, but for some reason he was sure she knew.

"How do you know all that?"

The smile on her mouth turned into a playful pucker forcing her cheeks to dimple on both sides. "You handed me my scarf with your left hand. You don't have a ring."

"You felt for a ring?"

"I dropped the scarf on purpose. You smelled good."

That made him laugh aloud. "Okay, keep going."

"I've held the arms of many people. I'm five-five, so I know my heights from there."

"I'm six-three."

"I was close."

"My education?"

"You have an accent, but your words have a refined quality to them. I'd guess you can speak more than one language."

"My father speaks French, and so does my aunt. I've always known both."

Courtney nodded slowly as though she were collecting her reward for knowing so much.

Tyler leaned in closer. "Okay, those are all logical. How do you know I have blue eyes?"

"That one was a guess, but I was right. You just told me."

"You have quite a talent."

Courtney turned her head toward the window. "You also seemed lost."

"I beg your pardon? How would you know that?"

"I could feel it. It felt as though you could use some company, and I sure know I could."

Tyler wasn't sure how this woman could tell so much about him, but she had a keen sense of the world around her.

The last passenger to board the plane was a soldier in uniform. As he passed by their row he looked down at Courtney as if he knew she'd be there, and then he continued to his seat which Tyler noted was the seat he was to have occupied.

As the doors were secured the pilot came over the speaker.

"Ladies and Gentlemen, we will be starting our flight shortly. I wanted to inform you that we have the honor of flying a vet home to his final resting place today."

The air in the plane grew thick and Tyler could hear the many gasps and even sobs which had come from that announcement. He turned toward Courtney who had gripped her hands in front of her, and pressed her forehead to her white knuckles.

"Are you okay?" Tyler asked.

She lifted her head and he could see the tears streak down her cheek from under her sunglasses. Hesitantly she nodded.

"I'm finally getting to make the journey to take my brother home."

Tyler let out a long breath and watched as this woman, he'd just met, turned her face toward the warmth of the sun coming in through the small window.

Tyler had gained a sister and felt like his world had ended.

Courtney had lost a brother, and yet was thankful to be with him on his final ride home.

Tyler rested his head against the back of his seat. His life didn't make any more sense than it had three years ago when he'd left Nashville. But at least when he got there, his brother, sister, and his parents would be there.

What was there for Courtney?

CHAPTER 2

*C*ourtney sat with her face toward the window as the plane took off. The trip was already harder than she'd imagined and now she'd involved a man she didn't even know into her misery.

Tyler was sitting with his face forward, his hands in his lap, but Courtney knew his eyes were on her. She'd spent most of her life with someone keeping watch over her with their peripheral vision.

Usually someone on a plane seated next to her would be stiff —rigid as though they were worried about having to help her, the poor blind girl. But that wasn't the vibe she was getting from Tyler. He was just waiting until she spoke again.

"I suppose the weather will be getting warmer soon. Nothing quite like Nashville in the summer."

She heard the laugh that rattled in his throat. "There is this enormous boulder in the middle of a stream on my grandmother's property. My brother and I would spend hours laying on that rock when it was hot." He let out a soft breath. "When it would get hotter, you'd stick your feet back into the water."

"That sounds nice."

"Oh, it was—is. She has horses and a garden. So you'd spend time on the rock and then run through the field to the horses and go for a ride. We'd cut my mother bouquets of flowers from my grandmother's rose garden and my grandmother would never complain."

"I love roses."

She knew he'd turned his head to face her. "Do you?"

Courtney nodded. "My brother was actually the last person to buy me some when he was on leave last year. They were in an enormous arrangement. If I think about them hard enough, I can still smell them, feel them."

"Feel them?"

"Yes. The satin soft touch of their petals. I know they were red because he told me, but I imagined they were pastel."

"So you get to imagine things look just as you'd like them to?"

"I guess I do."

"Pastel roses are pretty."

She smiled. "I always thought they were."

Courtney heard him run his hand over his cheek and he was due for a shave, though she was sure he was stunning with the slight bit of beard growth. But she also was sure he was thinking.

"So you know pastel? Does that mean you have had sight?"

The whole fact that this man was talking to her as if she were perfectly normal had her heart fluttering. Usually when she did the drop the scarf bit with a good smelling man, he wouldn't even acknowledge her after she'd get her scarf back. More often, some old lady would end up picking it up.

But Tyler was different. He didn't seem put off by her lack of sight. Well, okay, he was polite. The flight was only a mere few hours. He might walk right off that plane and never care to look back. But at this point, what did she have to lose?

"I was eight when I lost my sight. I remember many things, many people. I'm lucky that way. I can remember colors."

He leaned in toward her and she could feel his body heat as he grew closer. "I'll bet the colors you see are much more vivid."

She tried not to sigh, but it was damn near impossible.

"My favorite color was pink. I see it most often. I can see light and dark."

"As in day and night?"

She smiled. "Yes."

"I don't know that I've ever had a favorite color."

"I would guess your favorite color would be blue."

"Like my eyes."

On a laugh she said, "Yes, just like that."

"Why blue?"

"Because you're easy and cool."

"Cool?" That had actually made his voice rise. "Oh, I don't know about that."

"You are. You're cool with people. Not as in you're cold to them, you're cool around them. They don't ruffle your feathers too much."

"Around strangers I suppose."

"But around family?"

She felt the seat next to her bounce a bit. That had hit a nerve.

It took a moment, but she heard him take the breath to tell her about his family.

"I have a wonderful family. But I've been on a bit of a self-exploration of sorts for the past few years."

Courtney nodded. "You needed to find yourself?"

"Yes," he said with an excited pitch to his voice as if she understood exactly what he meant. And didn't she? Hadn't she been doing much of the same herself?

"What made you decide you needed to find yourself? Was your college major not what you thought it would be?"

He laughed. "No. I found out I had a relative I didn't know about."

Courtney tucked her hair behind her ear casually. "That could be very broad. You have a cousin you'd never met?"

"A sister."

"Now that is a bit more intriguing."

"I suppose. She's wonderful actually. The last time I was back in Nashville was for her wedding."

"So you're friendly with her?"

"Yes."

"And you're close to your parents too, so this is why she is a problem."

There was a chuckle from him. "You're good at this."

"I've had a lot of practice."

Tyler shifted in his seat and she could feel hers move as he adjusted. "My mother never told me. I didn't know I had a sister. I didn't know she'd been involved before my dad. Nothing."

"Your feelings are hurt."

"Were. I'm going with were."

Courtney was still going with *are*, because he wasn't over it yet. But she'd give him credit for heading back home to try and make amends with it.

"Your sister found your mother then?"

"Yeah. She'd hired some guy to find out about her. She'd been told her whole life that her birth mother died."

"That would be horrible."

"Her birth father was crazy." The word played on his voice as though he were frightened of him too.

"So her mother, your mother, gave her away to keep her from him?"

"Exactly. He'd tried to kill them both. She thought it was better if she lived somewhere else—with someone else. As someone else."

Tyler's voice had grown distant as though he was hearing this story for the first time and it meant something to him. She'd continue to talk then if he was having an ah-ha moment.

"Why would he try to kill them? I don't understand why people just don't walk away. It happens often enough."

"He was some rich—I don't know what he was," he said as if he realized there was part of the story missing. "I just know he invested in things. He'd invested in a build my father was building and that was how he found out my mother didn't die."

"I can't even imagine."

"Neither can I."

She felt Tyler turn and she knew someone was there.

"Courtney, can I get you a drink?" Celia asked.

"A Bloody Mary would be wonderful," Courtney answered.

"And for you, sir?" Celia asked Tyler.

"I think that sounds good. I'll have one too." Tyler turned back to Courtney. "I think I've only had one Bloody Mary in my life. It was at a bar on Broadway where my cousin was playing."

"In Nashville?"

"Yeah." He relaxed back again. "I can't remember where."

"Your cousin is a musician?"

He laughed. "Yeah she is. She and her husband actually." He turned and she could feel his arm brush hers. "Have you ever heard of the Wrights?"

"The singing duo?"

"Yep."

"Clara and Warner Wright?" She turned so their faces were close.

"That's them."

"You're kidding me? Clara Wright is your cousin?"

He moved and she heard him lower her tray table and then his. "Clara's dad is my mom's brother."

"What a small world."

"Her brother is married to my sister."

Courtney dropped her shoulders. "The sister you just found out about is married to your cousin?"

Tyler laughed. "My mom, my aunt, and my uncle are all

adopted. So my cousin and sister share no blood relation. And they fell in love before anyone knew who she was."

"That's a very romantic story."

Courtney heard the rustle of drinks being set on the tray, and Tyler adjusted them. "I suppose it is romantic. I've never been one for romance. I guess I never gave it enough time."

"How do you give romance time? It just happens, right?"

He laughed again. "You're asking the wrong guy about that."

Courtney turned so she faced him fully. "Are you telling me you've never had a girlfriend? Or a boyfriend?" She didn't think the latter was his way, but she'd feel it out.

He'd picked up his drink and she was very certain he'd choked on the sip he'd taken when she asked.

"Boyfriend?"

"Just being P.C."

He cleared his throat. "I've dated a few girls over the years. But nothing ever clicked."

She felt a click between them. It was probably the altitude so she was certainly going to keep it in check.

CHAPTER 3

*C*ourtney reached for the Vodka bottle.

"It's on your right. Straw is between the cup and the can of mix."

She clenched her teeth, not because he was telling her where she'd find things, but because she wanted to keep her mouth from falling open. He'd actually not jumped over himself to do it for her. He'd given her direction and she wondered if he believed in love at first sight because she was beginning to.

"With all of these relatives you're learning about, you don't happen to have a blind one do you?" she asked as she opened the Bloody Mary mix.

"No, why?" His voice had a hint of humor.

"You handle me differently than most people who just met me do. You treat me normal."

"You are normal," he replied quickly and that had her heart racing.

"Thank you."

She heard the ice in his cup against his lips as he drank. If she said much more, she was sure he'd be trading seats with her traveling companion, but she didn't want that. Though the solider assigned to fly with her brother was a nice man, she'd rather keep Tyler as company.

"Tell me about your brother," Tyler said as she began to pour her drink.

Courtney could feel her hands shake. She let out a breath. "I will. Will you make this for me? I seem to be a little shaken up."

"My pleasure," he said softly, and she was damn near sure it just might be his pleasure.

When he'd mixed her drink, he set it in her hand. "There's still half the mix and half the Vodka left."

"Thank you." She took a sip and it was perfect. It was just what she'd needed. "Fitz was wonderful." She didn't know how else to say it.

She sipped her drink again and then let out a relaxed sigh. "He was younger by four years. So there were times when he was a royal pain in my butt, but he still took care of me—especially after I lost my sight."

Courtney rested her head back against the seat, closed her eyes, and smiled. "Oh, I can't tell you how many times he got suspended for defending me. But he always stood up for me. He took really good care of me."

Tyler placed his hand on hers and gave it a squeeze. "I'm so sorry for your loss."

"Thank you. He was where he wanted to be. I can't be sad. But damn I'm going to miss him. Especially since we shared a house. Though he wasn't ever there. But it was ours."

"You know, I'll be around. If you ever need to talk, you could call me."

A warmth filled her body from head to toe. "You mean that?"

"Of course."

A smile played on her lips. She didn't want to seem eager, but she couldn't help it. "I'd really like that."

"Do you have your phone? I can put my name into it."

Courtney reached into her pocket and took out her phone. She powered it up and handed it to him.

A few moments later he handed it back to her. "It's in your contacts."

"Did you tag it under cute guy on airplane?"

He laughed. "I'll let you do that."

And she figured she just might.

As THE FLIGHT began its descent, Tyler noticed a change in Courtney. She hadn't said anything for nearly twenty minutes. Her fingers were entangled on her lap, and she kept her head toward the window.

The closer she got to home the harder it was. He knew what she was feeling.

As soon as the plane landed, the pilot asked everyone to please remain seated until the soldier and his escorts were off the plane.

Courtney turned her head toward him and placed her hand on his arm. "Thank you for the company."

"It was my pleasure."

The soldier who was meant for Tyler's seat was standing next to them in the aisle. Both Tyler and the other passenger stood and moved out of the row so that Courtney could pass by. As she did, Tyler reached for her.

"Don't forget. Anytime," he said hoping that she'd actually call him.

She nodded, took the arm of her traveling companion, and headed for the door. The pilot stood outside the cockpit and gave his condolences to Courtney and then a hug. A moment later, she was gone.

Tyler sat back down in the seat Courtney had occupied. He could see people gathered around the luggage conveyor. Soon Courtney was there with her companion and what he assumed were her parents.

The casket, draped with a flag, was taken from under the plane and loaded into the hearse that waited next to the family. Tyler was sure his heart and his breath stopped as he watched. Courtney had to be hurting worse than he could ever imagine.

Her father put his arm around her shoulders and held her mother's hand in his as they walked to a black SUV which also waited. Then Courtney stopped, turned back to the airplane, and waved.

Tyler knew it was meant for him and he waved back, though he caught himself, and knew she hadn't see it.

He sat back in his seat and closed his eyes. Before he even stopped to see his own mother and father, he would go by his sister's house. At that moment, he knew he needed to see her first.

CHAPTER 4

A rental car made Tyler feel a little more at home. At least he wasn't arriving at his sister's house in a cab.

When he pulled up to the house, he let out a long breath. There were cars parked everywhere, and the car parked in front of the house was his father's.

Tyler realized it was Sunday. That meant a large family meal and time together. Since Ed owned his grandparents' house, and their grandparents now lived in a retirement community, that meant those dinners were still held where the tradition had started.

If he drove on, no one would ever know. He had a hotel room lined up. If he walked into his father's office tomorrow, no one would be the wiser.

Tyler slowed the car, saw a parking space, and decided now was the time. His entire family was in that house. Courtney was somewhere in Nashville mourning.

Tyler parked his car and climbed out. Sucking in the air filled him with home. This was where he was rooted. This was where he belonged. No matter where he'd traveled in the past three years, or what job he'd done, or sight he'd seen, nothing compared to Nashville.

He was still considering getting back into the car and driving away, when the front door opened and his cousin Clara stepped out onto the front porch with her cell phone to her ear.

He couldn't hear the conversation, but there was a smile on her lips. Could that mean her husband wasn't inside, but on the phone?

For a moment he watched her absent mindedly play with her hair and laugh easily. He'd followed her career, bought her music, and watched her on TV. She'd done very well for herself. Tyler was proud of her.

Then, as if maybe she knew he was watching, she lifted her head and looked in his direction.

"Oh, my, God! Warner, I have to call you back. Tyler's home!" She pushed a button on her phone and ran toward him.

His heart swelled in his chest as she ran across the street with her arms already stretched wide.

"Oh! You're home!" She called at him as she jumped into his waiting arms and wrapped her arms around his neck.

He fell back against the car, his cousin in his arms. "I'm back," he laughed as she gave him a squeeze.

"No one told me."

"No one knows. Well now you do."

She looked him over from head to toe and then her eyes settled on his. "You're home for good. I can see it. You're back."

Tyler nodded. "I'm back."

"Your mother is going to be so happy."

Clara took his hand and started for the door, but he gave hers a tug and stopped.

"I think I should wait—until tomorrow."

Clara turned and narrowed her eyes on him. "Wait? Why would you do that?" She studied him a moment longer. "You came here to see Darcy."

"You've always been good at reading people."

"It's a gift."

Tyler tucked his fingers into the pockets of his jeans and rocked back on his heels. "I owe a lot of people apologies. But I need to start with Darcy. She came into our lives and I ran away."

"No one blames you for that. How could we?"

"I blame me. She didn't deserve that." He expelled the guilt building in his chest on a breath. "My mother didn't deserve that."

Clara moved back to him and rested her hands on his arms. "Both of them are inside. If you're back, you have a lifetime to apologize to them. Come in now and be with us. Part of us. We all love you and miss you."

Did he have it in him to walk through that front door? His mind wandered back to Courtney and how she dropped her scarf. The world was invisible to her, sight wise, but she trusted the feelings that surrounded her. Tyler knew the feelings he was having. Everyone he held dear was across the street, inside that house.

If Courtney trusted the whole world, couldn't he trust his gut and walk inside?

Clara grabbed hold of his hand and gave him a tug. "I think I just need to make the decision for you. Let's go."

He took her hand willingly and held it as they crossed the street.

"Your new single is awesome," he said and she smiled at him.

"My husband is a writing genius."

"He's that. Where is he?"

She slid a look his way. "Don't tell anyone, but he has a solo project. He's working on it very hard."

Tyler stopped. "Solo? Why would he do that? You're a team."

"We are. And my first love was Arianna's theater. I'm going back there to do Annie again."

"You're too old for that," he teased.

She laughed. "Ms. Hannigan now."

"Okay. You're old enough for that. Maybe too old."

She slapped him on the shoulder. "That's funny." Clara sighed and dropped her shoulders. "I want a baby too. And you can't have that perfect family life I had if you're on the road."

"You're having a baby?" His voice lowered as he looked at her.

"No. I'm just planning it. But I think if I'm near home working, it'll happen. Being on the road is stressful."

"Then it'll happen when the time is right."

"Just like you coming home."

CHAPTER 5

$\mathcal{A}$s Clara opened the front door, Tyler heard all of the voices of his loved ones. Clara had been right. It was the right time.

They stepped through the front door of the home he'd come to when he was little. The smells were the same. The noises were the same.

He knew if he walked in further, his grandfather would be in the same place and his grandmother would be in the kitchen. They might not live there anymore, and it might be Ed and Darcy's house, but he knew that much wouldn't have changed.

Clara turned to him as he stood by the front door. "Aren't you coming?"

"I just needed a moment."

And one moment was all he'd gotten.

"Who are you talking..." His cousin Christian passed by the front hallway. "Well I'll be damned."

He moved to him nearly as quickly as Clara had and pulled him in for a hug.

"Why didn't you tell us you were coming?" Christian asked as he pulled back.

Tyler noticed the wedding band on Christian's finger and guilt punched him in the stomach. He'd gone to Ed and Darcy's wedding because he felt he had a vested interest in it, but he'd neglected to be there for Christian's.

"It was a last minute decision," he said on a partial lie.

"C'mon. Get in here." Christian slapped him on the shoulder and walked back toward the living room. "Look what I found in the hallway."

Tyler winced. This was it.

Before he even made it to the living room, the hallway had been flooded with relatives. Uncle Carlos and Aunt Madeline hugged him as did his cousin Avery and her mother, Aunt Simone. Uncle Curtis somehow managed to pull him through and into the room where his grandfather sat in the chair he always had in that same place.

He was nearly ninety-five, but there was still a vibrant man looking up at him. "Well, look who came home." He patted Tyler's hand.

"It's nice to be home, Grandpa."

But the sound of a woman sniffling caught his attention and he looked up to see his mother standing in the doorway, his father behind her with his hands on her shoulders.

She said nothing, only opened her arms to him and he went to her.

His mother enveloped him in a hug and held him. His father wrapped his arms around both of them.

"I'm sorry I was gone for so long," he said into his mother's ear, but for both of them to hear.

"You're home? Are you really home?"

He could feel her sob against him and the pain of what he'd done was sharp. "I'm home."

The sobs from his mother came harder, but he'd been prepared for that. She'd done the same when he made the very quick trip for Ed and Darcy's wedding.

His mother pulled back. Her dark eyes were red from the tears which had come so quick and strong.

"You didn't tell me you were coming," she said with a soft, wavering voice.

"I didn't really know." He took her hands in his and looked down at her. "I hurt you and I can never say I'm sorry enough. You gave me a wonderful life and I held a decision you made against you. I never should have done that."

The tears started again. "You forgive me?"

"I did that the moment I learned about it. I had to learn to forgive myself for what I felt about it."

She pulled him back into her arms. "I'm glad you're home."

Tyler noticed his brother and sister standing in the doorway to the kitchen. Spencer had his arm around Darcy's shoulders, and she sobbed.

As his mother pulled back, Tyler went to them. These were the two people he shared his blood with and he had abandoned them.

Tyler was immediately pulled into their embrace.

"I let you guys down. I'm sorry. I want to make it up to you."

He could feel Darcy sob, just as their mother had, and even Spencer sniffed back tears.

Darcy stepped back and looked at him. "We have time. We have all the time in the world to get to know each other."

"You didn't deserve this from me. I shouldn't have left."

"You needed to do what was in your heart to make it all okay. But you standing here in my house makes me think that perhaps you've made amends with it all."

"I think I have."

THE HOUSE SEEMED SMALLER with so many people there. The dining room table had been extended and two more card tables added. His grandmother and grandfather sat where they had all the years he'd grown up eating family dinners there.

Though they'd asked about what he'd done while he wasn't in Nashville, they didn't focus on him the entire time and that made him more comfortable. He supposed in time they'd all corner him and ask him about his years away. But for now, he was happy to be surrounded by them.

Uncle John passed the basket of rolls to Tyler. "Do you need a place?" he asked.

"I guess I do. I have a room reserved at a hotel for tonight..."

"You what?" His mother's voice broke as she questioned his plans. "You never have to do that when you're in town. For the night or permanently."

His father rested his hand over his mother's.

"I know, Mom," he said softly. "This was hard. I needed a night to think."

Spencer laughed. "You needed a night to think and you came here?"

Tyler swallowed hard. "Well, I'd forgotten about dinner on Sundays. I came directly here to see Darcy."

Darcy pursed her lips and batted her moist eyes. "You know, Tyler, I have some wine chilling in the refrigerator out back in the garage. Why don't you go with me and we'll bring it in."

She stood from the table as everyone watched. Then, their eyes turned toward him. Tyler stood and followed her to the kitchen and out the back door.

When he reached her, Darcy was on the back step taking a deep breath of the air he'd missed so much. She didn't turn to him.

"Why did you come here first?" she asked.

"You're my sister, and I forgot to embrace what a wonderful thing that is."

She turned now, her eyes shimmering from lingering tears in the low light of dusk. "You're okay with that now?"

Tyler nodded. "What my mother—our mother—went through was horrible. She did what she did to protect you. She didn't say anything to the rest of us to do the same."

Darcy reached out a hand to him and he took it. "I love you and Spencer. When I fell in love with Ed, I thought I'd need to find my birth mother. I thought that my entire life had become whole when I landed in this family. And to find out I belonged," she sighed. "You can't imagine what that did for me."

"You do belong."

"And so do you. It hurt when you left. It hurt Regan and Zach. Spencer has been lost…"

"And you?"

She batted her eyes quickly. "It hurt, Tyler. You hurt me by leaving."

"I'm sorry."

"You had to do it. I get it. But I felt as though, just as I was finding my family, I cost you yours. That's a heavy burden to have carried for these past few years."

Tyler pulled Darcy into his arms and held her against him. "I'm sorry I hurt you. I'll never do it again." He eased her back at arm's length and looked her in the eyes. "I came here first because I knew my mother and father would forgive me. I needed to make sure you would."

She dropped her shoulders. "Tyler, there was nothing to forgive." Darcy pulled him back to her and held him tight. "But I'm glad you're home."

"So am I," he said as his phone vibrated in his pocket and Darcy jumped back laughing.

"Word is out, huh? Everyone is looking for you now?"

He looked at the screen and smiled. "This is a woman I met on the plane."

Darcy laughed as she walked toward the detached garage and he followed. "You're picking up women?"

"She was escorting her brother home. His final trip home," he said softly.

Darcy turned. "He was…"

"A soldier. Killed in combat."

Darcy covered her mouth with her hands. "Oh, Tyler…"

"She's something too. Her name is Courtney. You'd like her."

She watched him carefully and then dropped her hands. "You like this woman."

"I do." He looked down at his phone. "She just texted me the information for his funeral."

"Are you going to go?" She began walking again with him following.

"I don't know. I just met her. Isn't that a little…"

"Wonderful." She pushed open the door. "Tyler, she's asking you to be there. That means she needs your comfort."

That did something funny to his heart rate. "You think I should go?"

"I do," she said as she opened the refrigerator and pulled out two bottles of wine. "I'd be happy to go with you if you'd like."

Tyler slid his phone back into his pocket and took the bottles from her. "No, but thank you. I'll sleep on it and then decide."

"You'd better sleep on it at Regan's. If you sleep in a hotel tonight, she might banish you for good."

He knew that was truth enough.

As they walked back to the house he thought of Courtney. He and Darcy seemed to have mended their very brief, but important relationship. Courtney had lost that relationship when her brother died.

She'd asked for him—reached out to him.

He couldn't let her down.

Besides, he really wanted to see her again.

CHAPTER 6

a night in his old bedroom was just what Tyler needed to mend his soul. A few more nights, and he might just be perfect.

His uncle and aunt still owned the house that they rented out, which Tyler had once lived in with Christian and Clara. It was available again, and was as much his home as his parents' house.

He'd borrow one of his dad's SUV's and go by his uncle's tomorrow and pick up the key. Tyler would also give a few more thoughts to attending Courtney's brother's funeral. Then he'd go buy a suit, because he already knew he was going.

TYLER'S UNCLE JOHN, who was retired and looked for any excuse to have something to do, met him at the rental property the next morning.

"I gave it a new coat of paint last summer. The sprinkler is on and the lawn mower is in the garage. With you here, you're in charge of that," John said as he pushed open the front door.

Memories flooded Tyler's head as he thought of the last time he'd stood in that doorway. He'd walked right out of it and took his truck loaded down with things and he left.

Though he'd tried to prepare everyone for his departure, he hadn't. Telling a cousin or two wasn't really getting the news out. Only telling his brother where he was, and swearing him to secrecy, that had been uncalled for. You didn't run in their family.

"I knew you'd want to stay here." His uncle turned and looked at him. "You do want to stay here, right?"

Tyler laughed. "Yes."

"Okay, good. I set up a bed in the bedroom and filled the fridge with food. I put beer in there too. Do you drink beer?"

That gave Tyler's heart a little squeeze. "I do."

"Beer is good when you've put in a hard day or need a minute to think."

Tyler was going to need a few of those—minutes to think.

His Uncle John handed him the key. "It's good to have you home. Everything feels right again."

"Thank you."

"Where's your truck?"

Tyler bit down on his lip. "I sold it a few years ago. I was working on an offshore oil rig and didn't need it."

"You? On an oil rig?"

Tyler nodded. "A Pierpont Oil rig."

John laughed when Tyler mentioned it. No one had talked much of his Aunt Simone's family since she'd moved to America permanently and married Tyler's Uncle Curtis.

"No kidding. Does Simone or Avery know that?"

Tyler shook his head. "No. I was just a guy on the rig."

John nodded as if he understood. Then he gave his shoulder a pat. "Let me know if you need anything. I'm sure you'll have plenty of company."

John smiled and let himself out the front door leaving Tyler alone to take it all in.

. . .

Tyler woke in the bed his uncle had set up for him. He'd awakened to birds outside his window in the house he now called home. Home. It was good to think about that.

There was coffee in the kitchen, but it wasn't going to make itself. Of course, the way his family worked, someone would probably stop by to check on him. If he stayed in bed just long enough, maybe the coffee would be made and brought to him. He chuckled to himself and opened his eyes.

As his eyes focused, he sat up and looked around. Hanging on the bedroom door was the suit Clara had helped him pick out the day before.

Tyler's heart ached. Courtney would say goodbye to her brother today. Tyler had only said goodbye to his family for a few years—for Courtney it was forever.

Planting his feet on the floor, he rubbed his hands over his face. There wouldn't be enough time to get a razor. How come he hadn't thought of getting one when Avery took him grocery shopping or Clara took him clothes shopping? They hadn't even mentioned his stubble, and that surprised him. But honestly, would Courtney care that he had a three day beard?

She hadn't texted him again. Maybe she'd had a change of heart. Maybe he shouldn't go.

No, on that plane he'd told her he'd be there for her if she ever needed him. Damn it, he was keeping his word.

Tyler parked nearly four blocks away from the church. Downtown on a Wednesday morning was bad enough. Add to it, that he could already see the crowd flowing into the church. Courtney Field's brother was a very important man.

As Tyler entered the church, he saw her. Already seated between her mother and father in the front pew, Courtney hadn't worn black. That struck him as odd. She wore a bright yellow dress, and she stood out like sunshine in the sea of darkness.

He followed the stream of people into pews. The pew in which he sat was a mere four from the back. Courtney would never know he was even there among those who came to mourn one Lance Corporal Gerald Fitzsimmons Field.

The casket of the honored Marine was draped with a flag. His picture was prominently displayed next to the casket, and an enormous floral wreath encircled it. Uniformed Marines stood off to both sides as if to still stand beside the Marine they had lost.

Tyler looked down at the card they had given him as he'd walked in. Lance Corporal Gerald Fitzsimmons Field, aka Fitz, was a mere twenty years and nine months old. Tyler swallowed hard. He wasn't much older at twenty-four. They'd both seen the world in different ways. Tyler's heart ached for what the young man might have seen in his twenty years and nine months.

Tyler's three year pity party was beginning to gnaw away at his gut. As the funeral started and the minister began to talk about Fitz, Tyler felt three years solidify into a lead ball and drop into the pit of his stomach.

Unselfishly, the man they were honoring graduated high school and joined the Marines. He fought for his country. He aided those in need. He died.

Tyler had been given a sister to love, and he'd run. His mother had to have gone through unspeakable battery for her to have given up a child she'd wanted. Tyler knew what kind of mother she was. She was attentive and kind. She was loving and strict with the discipline and it only made him and Spencer better people. And yet, he'd abandoned her to gather his own feelings over it.

Darcy had gone on a quest to find her birth family. She'd had a good upbringing, but she needed more. She got Tyler with that bargain, and he turned from her.

Tyler watched as Courtney's shoulders moved up and down, sobbing, he thought. Loss was a force you couldn't fight. It didn't give back what it took. Tyler had never had loss like that.

When the funeral concluded, the uniformed Marines moved to the pews and let each one empty and move to the family. Tyler thought it would be best to just sneak out. He'd text her later and tell her he was there, giving details so she'd know he was telling her the truth. Maybe in a week or so they could have coffee.

Tyler had contemplated too long. The Marine was at his pew and those around him began to file into the line to console the family.

Unlike his brother who could handle awkward situations with ease—which was why he'd be better at running their father's company—Tyler's nerves kicked up even more. He wiped his palms on his pant legs as he rounded that first pew and was within feet of Courtney and her parents.

There was a constriction in his chest as Courtney's mother looked at him with red rimmed eyes and a weak smile.

"Mrs. Field I'm…"

"Tyler." Courtney turned toward him and her cheeks lifted as her lips curled. "You came."

"I did," he said, his voice teetering on amusement and shock that she could pick him out of that many people by his voice, and he'd only said three words.

Courtney took her mother's arm. "Mom, this is the man I told you about. The one I flew to Nashville with. Tyler, this is my mother Mary."

"Tyler, it's very nice to meet you." Mary held her hand out to him.

"Likewise." He shook her hand. "I'm very sorry for your loss."

"Thank you," she said softly.

"Tyler," Courtney reached for his hand and he offered it. "This is my father Duane."

Mr. Field was dressed in military dress as well. That was

something Tyler hadn't expected. Tyler didn't know rankings, or what bars and pins meant, but Duane Field had plenty of them.

Tyler held his hand out to shake her father's. As expected, her father's grip was firm as he looked down at Tyler, who himself stood at six-foot-three.

"Sir, it is nice to meet you. I'm very sorry about the loss of your son."

"Tyler." He repeated his name. This was something Tyler had learned from his father. It gave him some authority and helped in remembering the name. "My family appreciates you coming. Courtney says you were a great support to her in a very dark time."

"Thank you, sir."

Courtney reached for him again and pulled him back to her so that she could whisper in his ear. "There is a reception after internment. It's at our home. I'd like you to come."

Tyler patted her hand. "Should I find you at the cemetery?"

Courtney nodded. "I'll have my mother watch for you."

Mary nodded as well and Tyler leaned into Courtney, and kissed her cheek. "I'll find you."

CHAPTER 7

*C*ourtney's mother took Courtney's hand and gave it a squeeze.

"You were right. He is cute," she whispered.

"I'm glad he came. I hope it's okay I invited him to the house."

"Of course it is." Mary turned and Courtney knew another wave of people were there, saying the same thing—*I'm sorry for your loss. He was such a great man. Let me know if there is anything I can do for you.*

Tyler had come through for her. Courtney felt warm. It was the first time she'd felt that warmth since she disembarked that plane.

Tyler Benson was good people. She appreciated that.

Courtney stood by her parents' sides for at least another twenty minutes before they followed her brother's casket out to the waiting hearse. She could smell the sprays of flowers which her mother had meticulously explained to her in detail—mostly to keep herself calm, Courtney knew.

There were whispers she could hear around the church. *He was too young. It's so sad. What will they do?* And always there was the, *It looks like Courtney's doing well with her disability.*

Those were the only times she wished she had her sight so she could look right at that person and give them a what for.

Disability her ass. Did they smell the flowers? Did they all know they shook her hand differently and a million things were said in that touch? Did they know she knew their voices? Each voice had a tone and likewise an underlying tone. Oh, her disability had her seeing things sighted people never would see. And one of those things she saw was that Tyler Benson had been one of the most genuine people at that funeral. Thank God he came.

When Courtney had sent the text, she wasn't sure Tyler would come. He'd never replied, and she'd finally decided the number was wrong, or he just wasn't as interested as she thought he'd been.

She got that. After all, she'd been without her sight for nearly eighteen years. That was a lot of time to learn about people. Though she was still learning, she felt as though she had quite a grasp on it.

Courtney stood with her mother and father as they loaded her brother's casket into the hearse. She felt her father's body stiffen as she held his arm. Courtney assumed he had cried in private. Who wouldn't when your son died? Especially when Fitz died. But as her mother sobbed to her side, Courtney knew her father was at attention saluting his son.

The air was changing. She could feel it. The rain would hold off until her brother was buried and his mourners had gone on. The rain would be soft and it wouldn't last long. It would be as if the world cried for him—her—them.

Her father's arm folded for her to take his elbow and they began to walk. The cars had started their engines and she could feel the heat that produced on her legs.

They stopped and she could feel another person with them. As her father said, "Thank you," she knew it was the driver who had opened their door.

Her mother moved to the car first.

"The car is right at the curb. You won't need to step off. About four steps ahead," her father said.

Courtney gave him a nod and he placed her hand on the door of the car. She guided herself toward the opening and slowly moved until her foot was in the car and she could lower down to the seat.

Again, she was lodged between her stiff father and her sobbing mother. Another hour and she could be with Tyler, she thought. She could use some friendly conversation.

Her father moved on the seat next to her. This meant he was going to turn to her and talk to her. She was more than familiar with his precise body language.

"Do you think a yellow dress was really the most appropriate thing to wear?"

"Fitz bought it for me. He said I was his sunshine. I thought it was very appropriate."

"And why was Tyler here?"

She gave her father props for remembering his name. "Because he's a kind man and he knew it would mean a lot to me."

"Does he know who you are?"

Courtney left her hands palms down on her legs, but the desire to bunch the fabric of her dress in her fingers was almost too powerful. "He knows I'm Courtney Field. He knows my brother died."

Her father shifted against the back of the seat. "I don't want some gold digger looking for an easy prey."

Now the fabric began to grip to her fingertips and her mother must have noticed as she rested a hand on Courtney's arm.

"His name is Tyler Benson. I've Googled him. He's not a gold digger, Daddy."

"So who is he?"

"He is the heir to Benson, Benson, and Hart."

A satisfied noise hummed from her father's throat. "Real estate development."

"Right. And a nice man."

"You like him?"

Courtney let her shoulders drop. "I've met him one time. He was very nice. And yes, I like him. But that doesn't mean anything. It was nice to have someone to talk to on the plane."

"You had an escort. You dismissed him."

"I did. And I had a much nicer flight."

The hum from her father was back, but then the car slowed. Perhaps he'd let it be for now. As for her, she sure as heck was going to find out about Tyler Benson. She did like him, and she'd like to find out just how much.

CHAPTER 8

*T*yler parked his car on a narrow path in the cemetery. Again, he was going to have to walk quite a bit to get to the site, but that was okay. He needed some time to clear his mind.

Courtney's parents had been gracious, but her father didn't trust him. Though, Tyler was sure, her father didn't trust anyone.

The family had already arrived graveside and were seated by the time he'd made it to them. He stood at the back of the crowd of mourners, but he watched Courtney.

The dress she wore was even brighter now in the sunshine. It gave her a glow he wasn't sure he'd noticed before.

Her mother dipped her head to her and whispered in her ear. Courtney gave her a nod and then smiled.

What was it about her? Why had he captured her attention? He'd been told he had a good face, a nice voice, and he'd had a couple women—only a couple—tell him he was nice to wake to. But Courtney couldn't look at him and think he would be someone to show off to Mom and Dad. She had to know from her gut. And that was why she'd asked him to be there, right? In her gut Courtney thought he was a good guy?

Tyler on the other hand, had his sight. He could see how glorious the yellow dress made her look. How it made her shine. Her long dark hair was pulled back in a low ponytail and she wore a very dainty necklace around her delicate throat.

Tyler looked down at his clasped hands. It was a funeral. It was her brother's funeral. Thoughts of how beautiful the sister of the deceased looked were not acceptable.

When he looked back up, Courtney's face was aimed his way. When he smiled, she smiled. How could she know that beyond a grave, and with sixty other people in front of him, he was looking at her? But she seemed to know.

Was that a power? A spiritual gift?

The minister asked everyone to bow their heads and he prayed for Fitz Field the Marine that Tyler would never know, but he'd mourn him. And in his own time, he'd thank him for the moment his death brought clarity to Tyler's own life. Perhaps he could do something with Fitz's memory to make his own journey worthwhile for others. That would be a thought. He could talk to his grandmother about that. She was the philanthropist sort. Something good had to come from this family's loss.

And as Tyler raised his head, he thought maybe it would be good for Courtney too. They could work together on it—get to know each other—feel this spark out.

As the service concluded, the mourners again paid their respects, so he moved toward the family. Mr. Field had gone to the Marines who had been there. He spoke to them and they were stiff and attentive. Mrs. Field smiled as he moved to them and Courtney's head lifted.

"Hi," he said as if he couldn't have thought of something better.

"Hi." Courtney smiled at him. "Will you come to the house?"

"If that's okay?" He looked to her mother who nodded.

"We'd be happy to have you," Mary Field offered.

"I can just follow you there."

"Oh, I'll go with you," Courtney said quickly. "I'll show you how to get there." She moved toward him and turned back to her mother. "Tell him I'm fine. I'll be there when you get there."

Instead of taking Tyler's arm she reached for his hand and interlocked their fingers. Her mother moved in and kissed her on the cheek.

"I'll let him know." Then Mrs. Field looked up at him. "Thank you for coming. We will see you at the house."

Tyler gave her a smile as she turned and walked away.

"Okay, let's hurry to your car," Courtney was already walking at a quickened pace.

Tyler enjoyed the feel of her hand in his, perhaps too much. That spark he'd been thinking about was erupting into a brush fire.

"I parked a long way down the road."

"Good. I haven't had a decent run in a few weeks."

"We're not running are we?" He asked thinking of the very uncomfortable shoes he had on.

She laughed and gave their hands a swing. "No, just keep walking and don't turn around."

Tyler did what she said. "Your father, is he going to be upset with me taking you home?"

"Yes." She let out a sigh. "Not because you're a man. Or because I like you. But because he's not in control and he thinks I need protection."

Tyler didn't stop, that would be equivalent to turning around, but he did give her hand a squeeze. "I know you don't know me, but I'd never hurt you or anyone else."

"I know," she said very matter-of-fact. "That's why I'm going to get in your car and show you to my house. That's why I'm holding your hand. Tyler, I might have only met you, but I have a keen sense of who you are."

It was a good thing, he thought, because somewhere he'd lost sense of who he was.

CHAPTER 9

Tyler had helped Courtney into the SUV and shut the door. Usually she'd have wanted to do it herself, another one of those things to prove to people that she could do it. But she knew Tyler did it as a gentleman, and not some person hell bent on helping the handicapped.

When he got in next to her, and shut the door, she turned to him. "Are you growing a beard? You didn't have one the other day."

He started the engine and gave a little chuckle. "I didn't mean to start one. I need a new razor and I was too busy moving in and getting settled to remember to get one."

"You bought a new suit."

She could feel his eyes on her, and her skin warmed. He chuckled again. "How do you know that?"

"It's stiff and smells new."

"My sister picked it out for me."

"It's a nice suit. She did a good job."

"How do you know it's nice? How do you know all these things?"

She smiled and faced forward. "It's almost scary, huh?"

"A little, but I'll admit, exciting."

Now she laughed. "Exciting?"

"Sure. To know someone can peg almost everything about you without seeing you is crazy. Okay, I know you guessed on the eye color, but you even got that right."

"Let's call it my superpower. Blind Girl."

The car went silent, but then she heard what she thought was a slight laugh. Okay, he was warming up to her humor.

"I suppose I should tell you which way to drive," she interrupted the silence.

"It would help, but I have a feeling I could drive for hours before I thought to ask because I enjoy your company."

His words rattled in her. "I wouldn't have thought I was good company on the two times you've been with me."

"Well then, I'll assume that means that next time you'll be even better company."

"Next time?" Her voice actually cracked.

"Sure. How about dinner?"

"I'd love it." She wanted to answer quickly so he knew she really did want to be with him. "I'm allergic to shell fish. Other than that I'm open to anything."

"Barbeque?"

"I like that a lot."

"Steve's Barbeque Pit and Beer."

She turned to him. "I love that place. Really? You'll take me there?"

"That's where my parents ate out for the first time. Minus the hot dog cart behind my dad's office."

Was it possible to adore a man so much she wanted to reach over and squeeze him? She wouldn't. She might not be able to see the traffic before them, but she knew better.

"I'd love to eat there with you under one condition."

"Okay, what's that?"

"Is that hot dog cart still there?"

He laughed. "Yes. Frank is gone but, well…" He stopped. "I've been gone long enough, I don't know if it's there. Frank sold it to another guy, but it was still called Frank's."

She could hear the drop in his voice. It was a drop of regret. He'd been gone too long to know if something constant was still around. She knew what he was feeling.

"Well, if it is there will you take me there too?"

Courtney felt him move and then he took her hand and locked their fingers together. She didn't want to gasp her surprise, but she wasn't sure she hadn't.

"I'll take you there. I promise. If not that one, another one."

Now butterflies filled her stomach. It was too good to be true that she'd dropped her scarf in front of a man so crazy wonderful. Something was wrong with him. There had to be something she hadn't noticed yet. Perhaps her father would tell her. He was good at pointing out the bad in everyone. He was skeptical about everyone he'd ever met.

Courtney let out a breath. She wasn't going to think like that. That was the way her father worked. Maybe, just maybe, Tyler Benson was as wonderful as he seemed.

"You need to tell me which way to go now," he said and she realized she'd gone quiet.

"I'd say just drive around until we run out of gas, but I suppose that would be frowned upon."

"If it was what you wanted, I do that."

Now the butterflies had begun to swarm in her chest.

"You would?"

"I would."

She told him where she lived, he let go of her hand, and she felt the car turn sharply.

"Could have missed the highway," he said on a laugh.

"Sorry."

"Don't be, but it's funny. That's out by where my grandmother lives."

"The one with the boulder in the stream?"

"Yeah, that one."

"We moved out there about ten years ago. Mom wanted a forever home, as she'd put it. She was done traveling with the Marines."

"So you've lived a lot of places."

"More than I can count," she said on a sigh. "But this is home."

"It's a nice area."

"Uh-huh." There was no reason for her to say more.

CHAPTER 10

Tyler followed Courtney's directions toward the house and they were very precise.

"Yep, you're about two miles north of my grandmother's place. I can't believe you lived so close," he said as he came to the road she'd directed him to turn on.

"Where did you grow up?"

"Not too far actually. About ten miles from here."

Courtney reached for his arm and traveled her hand down it until she found his hand. He let it relax as she took it in hers.

"I believe in fate. Do you?"

He swallowed hard. "I do."

"You and I were on that plane together. We both are going through things. We grew up in the same place."

"Fate?"

"Fate."

Tyler pulled into the very generous drive of a beautiful house encircled by trees.

"This is beautiful," he said.

"It doesn't have a boulder and a stream." She was smiling.

"I'm guessing it has other charms."

"Pull up and park just on the south side of the garage. There is some space."

He drove up the drive. "Will I be in anyone's way?"

"No. But this way you can get out when you're ready to leave."

He gave her hand a squeeze. "I'll stay as long as you'd like me to."

"You might as well park in the garage then." She chuckled, but the heat in his body spiked.

Tyler parked where Courtney had suggested and turned off the engine. The world around them went silent for a moment.

Courtney's hand was still in his and it trembled. He watched as she moistened her lips and took a breath—as if hers wasn't coming easy either.

"Tyler," she said breathy as she turned her head toward him. "I want to ask you something. When I'm done, you're free to go if you want to."

She swallowed hard and turned in her seat to fully face him.

"Did you only come to the funeral because I asked you to? Because you felt sorry for me?"

"No," he answered, his voice unsteady.

She shifted their hands so that their fingers interlaced. She'd raised the bar to be more intimate.

"Are you put off by my looks or the fact that I'm blind?"

"No." That answer was much quicker and sharp.

A smile began to form on her lips. "You do believe in fate?"

"I think I do."

"Would you be interested in kissing me?"

Every part of him wanted that, but he forced himself to control any part of him that would make him rush what he was feeling.

"Courtney, I'd be very interested."

She let out a long airy sigh and moved closer to him. "Will you kiss me then? Kiss me as if you've been dreaming about it for as long as you can remember."

Tyler lifted his free hand to her cheek. "That won't be so hard."

He moved to her slowly as she closed her eyes. Her lips parted in anticipation of his. As his mouth pressed to hers, he felt the sigh resonate from her.

The warmth of her mouth against his sent that brush fire into a full forest fire dwelling in his belly. Her lips parted further and their tongues met, exploding feelings in him he didn't realize he could even feel.

Thick air swirled around them as the kiss became more than just a friendly kiss. There was electricity in lips on lips, tongues searching, fingers clenching.

Courtney pulled back breathlessly. "They're coming," she said before he could hear the faint sounds of cars turning on the dirt road which would lead to the drive.

"I'll open your door." He moved to open his door.

"Tyler, that was very nice."

"Yeah it was."

She laughed at his near moan. "Can we do it again soon?"

"You can guarantee it." He gave her hand a pat and climbed out of the SUV.

COURTNEY TOOK the moment before Tyler opened her door to collect herself. Boys had been nice to her in the past and then ran like hell. Oh, she was no prude. She'd kissed plenty of boys—men. No one in the world kissed like Tyler Benson. The thought crossed her mind. He must have had a lot of women to know how to kiss like that. She didn't want to think she'd just be another—but honestly she didn't care at that moment. But she would in time.

Courtney had to remember that she was in mourning and he was helping her though that. She'd asked him to kiss her and he had. But, he'd wanted to, right?

The door opened to her side and Tyler touched her hand. Courtney turned in her seat, placed her hand on the door, and stepped out of the vehicle.

"I assume that's my parents coming up the drive."

Tyler chuckled as he shut the door behind her. "You're hearing is better than my sight. I can't see the car through the trees. But there are a lot of cars headed this way."

Instead of taking his elbow, she laced her arm through his. "Let's go in through the back. I don't feel like being right here when they get out of the car."

"Lead the way."

Courtney closed her eyes blocking the brightness of the sun and swallowed the feelings she was having. There was one thing she knew about Tyler Benson, he'd run away when things got too hard for him to deal with. Sure, he'd come home to mend that—but he'd run.

As Courtney led him around the house, she thought about what she was feeling. It wasn't unfamiliar to her. She'd felt these pains before. Very quickly she was growing attached to him—more than attached if she let herself be totally honest. This was something that could very well become—dare she think it—love.

But she couldn't let it take that form. Not yet. Fate or not, Tyler Benson might run. He knew nothing of her or her family. He'd yet to have to deal with her father beyond the pleasantries of condolences. He'd yet to have her mother break down in front of him. Heck, she hadn't even done that yet and she would. It was inevitable. No matter how strong Courtney was, she was fragile too.

At some point her lack of sight would get in their way. Courtney couldn't just jump in a car and head to him when he needed her. Fine, she'd admit it. She had a disability that stopped her from the things sighted people could do—such as hopping in a car and driving away. Perhaps she admired Tyler for getting to do that.

"Are you okay?" he asked as her hand had begun to shake.

"I have a lot on my mind."

"That's understandable." He took the step to the back door and she followed. "Just through this sliding door?"

"Yes. Maria will be right inside fussing over food."

"And Maria is?"

"My parents' cook. She's been with us for as long as we've lived here."

"I need to get me one of those," he joked and she smiled. She'd heard that a million times, but when Tyler said it, it didn't bother her as much.

Tyler opened the door and the scent of sauces and flowers filled Courtney's nose. Maria had been busy.

"Oh, Miss Courtney."

She stepped inside the kitchen and could hear Maria shuffling her feet toward her.

"Why did you come in the back? You will have guests."

"Maria, I have a guest. This is Tyler."

Maria didn't speak right away and Courtney knew she was sizing him up. She felt him move.

"It's very nice to meet you, Mrs..."

There was a hesitation hanging in the air. "Gonzales."

"Mrs. Gonzales. It is a pleasure."

She heard Maria giggle. He'd won her over. Tyler Benson was very good at that.

"You hungry? You both should eat. You look pale, Miss Courtney."

"I will. My parents just walked in."

Maria gave a low hum and she felt her move toward them. "She is scary, that one, with her ears. I did not hear them. Did you?"

Tyler chuckled. "No, I didn't."

"Hmmm. I better go to them." Maria shuffled off.

"You make friends easily," Courtney said as she led Tyler through the kitchen.

"I suppose I do. It's not that hard really."

"For some. You're that some."

Courtney led him by the hand to the entry. The sound of voices and steps resonated from the high walls. She heard her father's voice and knew he was speaking to a Marine. There was a different tone when he did so. Though, sometimes it wasn't unlike the tone he used with her.

"He was a good solider, sir," a man Courtney didn't know said.

"He was a fine one. A sacrifice a Marine understands," her father said with his cold, hard tone.

Courtney's stomach clenched and she grit her teeth. Where was that exceptional will inside her to approach her father and tell him what she thought of this sacrifice? He'd pushed Fitz into the military. From training when they were young, to military academies, to his death as a Marine fighting a war she didn't understand. That wasn't a sacrifice for the cause that was her brother he was referring to. Her flesh and blood. His flesh and blood.

She turned. "Tyler, get me out of here. Will you? Just take me."

"Okay," he said softly.

She took his elbow and he walked her back through the kitchen and out of the doors in which they'd come in.

When they were outside, Courtney could feel the warmth of the sun and see the bright sun as it was high in the sky now.

"Where do you want to go? There are some chairs out here or..."

"I want you to drive me away from here. I live in town. Or you can just drive around. Or..."

"I have somewhere. Do you trust me?"

She'd never trusted anyone more than she trusted him. "Yes."

CHAPTER 11

Tyler drove down roads he was familiar with. No one had noticed them leave and he had to wonder how long it might take before someone realized that the girl in the bright yellow dress wasn't standing out in the sea of black and gray.

Courtney was turned toward the window and she sobbed. Her father's words had hurt her—wounded her.

An anger brewed in Tyler—an anger that shouldn't be there. This family wasn't his. Their problems weren't his problems. But seeing Courtney's shoulders bob, just as he'd seen his mother's do when Tyler had returned for his sister's wedding—that's what hurt.

Tyler turned down one road, then another, and another. Not once did he hit paved ground. Then like a lighthouse in a storm, he saw the house he'd been heading toward.

Courtney turned her head. Her hair caught the breeze and her blew through the open window. "I hear a creek."

"Damn you have good ears."

She laughed through the last sob. "You'd be surprised what people whisper about."

He figured he would be.

Tyler drove up the drive and parked in front of the grand house that belonged to his grandmother. What would she think about Courtney? Oh, that was silly. He knew what she'd think. She'd think Courtney was as amazing as Tyler thought she was.

"Give me just a moment, okay?" He said and climbed out of the SUV. He wanted to see if his grandmother was home first.

TYLER RANG the doorbell and a moment later Audrey Benson pulled open the door. There she was as bright as a summer day. Her hair was white—and styled. Her dress was as bright as Courtney's, and bangles dangled from each wrist.

"Oh, Tyler!" She covered her mouth with her hand. She stepped to him and cupped his face in her hands. "Look at you. Just look at you."

"Hello, Grandma."

"When did you get home? Oh, come in. Come in. Clarice made some tea before she left for the store. Come in." She stepped back to let him through.

"Grandma, I have a guest. I'd like to invite her in if you don't mind." He moved in closer to his grandmother. "I think she could use a walk in your garden. Today was her brother's funeral."

His grandmother looked around him and toward the SUV in the driveway.

"You bring her in here. Of course you can walk in my garden."

Tyler kissed her on the cheek. "Thank you."

He walked back to the SUV and opened the door for Courtney.

"You brought me to your grandmother's house? The creek? I hear the creek," she said again.

"I did, and you do." He held his hand to her and she took it stepping out of the SUV.

She took his elbow. "You're very polite to people."

"That's how I was raised."

"Yes, well we all should be raised that way, but you—you respect everyone and their story. You didn't tell your grandmother I was blind."

"That doesn't define you."

She moved her hand from his elbow to his hand. "Don't forget me tomorrow."

"That'll never happen," he said as they approached the stairs. "There are four steps up to the door."

"Where did your grandmother go?"

He laughed. "I assume she's pouring us some iced tea and setting up a tray of cookies. This is what she does."

"I like her already."

TYLER GUIDED COURTNEY DOWN A HALLWAY. The house was very clean. Wood was polished. The floors were mopped. There were no piles or messes here, she was sure.

As they turned, Courtney could smell roses. These had been cut and arranged nearby. Perhaps more than one bouquet.

She heard glasses being filled. Liquid over ice and then it stopped and a crystal pitcher was set on a metal tray.

"Grandma, this is my friend Courtney."

She heard the shoes on the stone floor as a breeze of perfume moved to her. "Oh, Courtney." The woman took her hand. "It is so nice to meet you. I'm Audrey Benson. Tyler's grandmother."

"It is very nice of you to have me in your home. Thank you."

"Oh, honey, Tyler tells me today was your brother's funeral. I'm so sorry for your loss."

She sincerely felt as though the woman was sorry for her loss. Courtney appreciated that. "Thank you."

"He was young?"

"Twenty. He was a Marine."

She heard the sigh. "How brave."

Pride swelled in Courtney's chest. "Yes, ma'am, he was."

"Tyler, why don't you carry that tray out to the patio? I'll bring Courtney out."

He left her side and she felt herself stiffen. A moment later, Audrey was by her side offering her elbow.

Someone in this family had to be blind. How did they all know what she needed? Hopefully he wouldn't forget about her tomorrow. He'd said he wouldn't. She actually believed him.

"Tell me, Courtney, are you from Nashville?"

"Yes, ma'am. I was born here. But we moved all over the world. We returned to Nashville about ten years ago."

"You lived all over? How wonderful. Your father is military?" she asked as she stepped with Courtney through the patio doors.

"Yes."

She heard the tray being set down on a glass table. Then she felt him. He was by her side again.

"Do you want a patio chair or a lounge chair?" he asked.

"Where will you be?"

"Let's sit at the table. We'll have a glass of tea and then I'll show you around."

She tucked her hand into his and gave it a squeeze. "I'd like that."

As casually as could be, Courtney sat with Tyler and his grandmother in the afternoon sun. She quickly learned that Audrey Benson loved to talk. She loved to chat about the weather, the flowers, and how they were so much alike with their clothing choices. She'd learned that Tyler was named after his grandfather who had died before Tyler was born. And she learned that Audrey Benson had missed Tyler terribly.

Courtney had no idea how long they'd sat there, but her tea was gone, the sun had moved, and Audrey had yawned.

"I'm going to walk Courtney around, if that's okay. I'll bring the drink tray in with us."

"Wonderful. I think I'll go lay down for a spell. I have a dinner date," she said with pride.

"Do you? Who is taking my grandmother out to dinner?"

"A nice man I've been seeing from the club. His name is Charles. If you're too long, I'll be gone. But take your time."

Tyler moved and she heard him kiss her. "We will. If I miss you, I'll come back tomorrow."

Courtney heard Audrey pat Tyler's cheek. "You'd better. I have a lot of questions for you. You've been gone too long. And maybe you could shave."

Courtney couldn't help it, that had made her chuckle.

He heard Tyler kiss her on the cheek. "I love you, Grandma."

"I love you too. And Courtney…" Courtney raised her head when Audrey said her name. "You visit again. My Tyler likes you, I can see that."

"Thank you, ma'am."

Courtney heard Audrey walk away and close the door between the house and the patio.

"I like your grandmother. I see where you get your charm," Courtney admitted.

"Oh, you haven't met my parents yet," he joked and it forced her to swallow hard.

"Yet? You plan on introducing me to your parents?"

"I met yours."

"Well, yes, but…"

Tyler gathered her hands in his. "You think I'm going to run out on you don't you? You figure that I'm here to shower you with sympathy over your brother and then not give you another thought."

Courtney pushed her shoulders back. "You're the one who ran away from your family problems. I'm not your family, and I'm not your problem."

"Right, so why should I run?"

She felt the air grow thick around her. "No one sticks around in my life. Fitz was it. My mother, well she has her issues. My father is too busy being important to the military, and that keeps him from us. And Fitz is gone. Everyone else just treats me like I have a disease."

"You're blind. You're not tainted."

A tear fell and she pulled back a hand to wipe it away. "Sometimes they go hand in hand."

"Not in my world."

She felt his hand on her cheek and his body moved closer to hers until they pressed together. Courtney closed her eyes as she felt his breath nearing her skin.

Tyler's mouth came to hers, but it wasn't soft like before. This had a message. He accepted her—all of her.

She leaned into the kiss. His fingers tangled in her hair and his hand pressed into the small of her back.

Nothing had ever felt like this. Fate—she reminded herself. It was real.

When he broke the kiss, he didn't move. "In my world you're perfect."

It was possible that on the second day she'd been around Tyler, she'd tumbled into something she'd never tumbled into before. That thought was for another day. Today she buried her brother. Tomorrow she'd feel that. Right now she was going to wander the rose garden holding the hand of a man she didn't really know—yet.

CHAPTER 12

The moment Courtney stepped into the rose garden, she stopped. It was so fragrant she could only imagine that she was nearly buried in rose petals.

"What colors are there?" she asked.

"Roses? Oh, lots of red ones. Pink ones. A few purple. I think there are some orange too."

"Orange? Oh that's lovely."

"She has yellow too. The color of your dress. There are big ones and some tiny ones."

"Tea cup roses."

Tyler laughed as he gave her hand a squeeze, their fingers entwined. "I didn't know they had a name."

"They all have names. It would take me some time to feel them all, but I could name most of them."

"Perhaps you and my grandmother could do that someday—without me." He chuckled and she leaned into him.

"I actually think I would like that."

They moved through the rose garden, their hands held together, their arms swinging between them.

"How many horses does she have?" Courtney asked, her head moved toward the sun which was now dipping toward the west.

"I think she only has four left. The barn was once full. But she's too old to ride now, she says."

"I don't believe that."

"You figured her out pretty well, didn't you?"

"Remember my super power."

"Right." He nudged her. "Well, there are two horses that are hers and I think my Aunt Simone owns the other two and pays to have them, and Grandmother's, taken care of. She comes out and rides with my cousin Avery."

"Simone. That's a beautiful name."

"She's French."

"You said you had a French aunt."

"You remember everything don't you?"

"When it's important," she said swinging their hands grandly. "How did your uncle find a French woman?"

"Aunt Simone is my father's best friend. They grew up together. My father was sent to a boarding school outside Paris."

"That's why you and your father speak French?"

"*Oui,*" he said and she laughed.

"Having lived in many different cultures, I would think Paris and Nashville are worlds apart."

"Especially for her. Have you ever heard of Pierpont Oil?"

She stopped walking and turned her body to his. "Of course."

"That's her. She's the heiress to Pierpont Oil. Actually my cousin is, if she ever chooses it. My aunt and her father had a falling out when she fell in love with my uncle."

Courtney nodded and they began walking again. "I don't understand why parents can't accept when someone wants to be with someone or do something they just can't control. I mean, what business was it of his if she fell in love? I've met you and your grandmother. Something tells me your uncle is not a money seeking slob."

"He's a doctor."

She stopped again. "He didn't approve of a doctor?"

She felt Tyler's arms move in a shrug. "I guess everyone doesn't see eye to eye on that."

"Foolish," she said as the light shifted and she could hear the horses. They were walking into the stable.

Courtney closed her eyes and breathed in the scent of the hay and the animals. Freedom lived here. The kind you could ride with no one looking over your shoulder, on magnificent animal under you taking you fast in the wind or slow to relax.

She opened her eyes and she could feel Tyler's on her.

"Horses make you happy," he said.

"You've started reading people too?"

"I can see it. You're as bright as your dress right now."

She smiled. "Take me to one."

Tyler guided her to a horse. "This is Alistair. He's Avery's horse."

Courtney lifted her hand and the horse moved to her. "Oh, he's wonderful. Aren't you boy? Yes, you are a sweet thing. Very gentle."

"You can tell that by him sniffing you?"

"You can tell." She gave his neck a pat and lowered her hand. "Will you bring me again and we can ride?"

"Of course. I'm not very skilled at it."

"I am."

She felt Tyler's hand come to her waist and pull her to him. "I'll bet you are."

His mouth came to hers again and she swiftly wrapped her arms around his neck. As the heat of his mouth burned against hers the reality of the day hit her. She'd been sipping tea with his grandmother, wandering rose gardens, and loving on gentle horses. His kisses had nearly wiped her memories clean. But at that moment, she missed her brother.

She pulled back from him. "I'm sorry. It's just…I should…"

Tyler pulled her to him as she began to sob. "It's okay. I wondered when your strength would give out. You can cry all you need to. I'm right here."

And somehow, she always knew he would be.

CHAPTER 13

*T*yler looked up and he knew that the stars would be bright tonight. The sun was descending, the sky was clear, and this woman on his arm—well she was bright. He'd held her in the stables for nearly an hour. They'd sat on a bale of hay and she'd just cried. He knew she would. He was glad he was there for it.

When she felt as though she'd cried long enough, they began to walk.

"You're taking me to the creek," she said and her lips curled into a smile.

"It wouldn't be a complete trip if I didn't."

They walked through the field toward the creek. The heat wasn't as brutal as it had been that morning. A breeze had come through.

"Oh this sounds lovely." Courtney stopped and tipped her head back. "I thought it was going to rain today. I really did."

"The sky has no clouds."

"I know," she said and he was sure she did know.

When they reached the creek bank they stopped. "We have to cross into the water to get to the boulder."

She was grinning at him. "I've never been so excited to touch a rock in my life."

"We can leave our shoes here."

He bent down to untie his shoes and roll up his suit pants as she swiftly kicked out of hers.

"What's on your toenails?"

She wiggled her toes. "Lady bugs. I thought they'd go well with my sunny dress."

"You had lady bugs painted on your toes for your brother's funeral?"

"He'd have appreciated it."

"You're a wonder to me," he said standing and taking her hand. "I can't guarantee it isn't cold."

"Are you afraid of cold?"

He laughed now. "Not me."

"Good. Let's go." And with that she began to pull him toward the water.

Was she afraid of anything?

Tyler tried to get next to her and help her to the enormous boulder in the creek. "One side is lower so we can climb up." He walked her around the front of the enormous rock.

"This is exciting. Okay, how do I get up?"

"I've never done this in dress clothes," he said.

"We could certainly take them off."

Tyler choked out a cough. He hadn't expected that.

"I've kissed you, Tyler. I know you're not a prude. You don't get good at kissing like that without having had a lot of practice. That shouldn't have caused you alarm."

"Well it did." He moved in next to her. "Put your hands flat on the rock and I'm going to give you a boost."

She set her hands on the flat of the rock and he grabbed hold of her hips and lifted her until she was on the rock. Then he boosted himself up.

He scooted back and guided her to sit next to him.

She closed her eyes again. "I think I could sit here forever. It's so peaceful. The water. The breeze. The horses in the back. The sway of the fields."

"I don't think I'll ever look at things the same way now. You see more than I do and I'm looking at it."

"Close your eyes then," she said and he did.

It was then he could hear the water lapping up the side of the rock, the grasses in the field swayed, and the horses sounded as if they were having a conversation back at the stable. The air was shifting and even through closed lids, he could see it was getting darker.

"Do you see it all now?" she asked.

He reached for her hand and brought it to his lips. "I do."

"You've been very generous with your time today. I'm sure there were a million other things you needed to do."

He interlaced their fingers. "Today you were my priority."

"I appreciate that." She let out a sigh. "Tomorrow things will be different. I suppose I'll have my mother on my front step wanting to clean out my brother's things."

"Seems there would be plenty of time for that."

"You'd think. But I know her."

Tyler opened his eyes and turned his head to look at her. "I should probably get you back."

Her head dipped. "I don't want to go back. Would you mind taking me home? To my home, I mean. It's in the city, so if that's a problem I can take a bus."

He let out a snort. "Even if it were far away, it wouldn't be a problem. I live in the city too. It won't be an issue."

"You live in the city? I didn't realize you'd kept a place."

"I didn't. My aunt owned a house and would rent it out when she lived in New York. When my mom moved back to Nashville, she lived there, and when my uncle got divorced he moved in with her."

"It's sort of a family rental?"

He laughed. "Oh, yeah. It gets better. So my aunt moved back and her husband, who was the caretaker of the property for my dad's company," he shook his head. "Are you keeping up?"

"Of course. Your uncle worked for your father and they looked after the house and he lived there."

"Damn, you're better than I'd have been at that."

"I don't have a very significant distraction. I'm sure if I were looking at your handsome face, I wouldn't have caught any of that. But go on. I'm very intrigued about this house."

"Okay. Well, they got married and the house was for rent again. My cousin Christian lived there and then my sister moved in. That was before we knew she was my sister." It still sounded like a damn soap opera to him, even if it really wasn't one. "I lived in the basement until I left on my trip."

"Your trip of self discovery."

"Yeah," he said with the regret that he carried with it. "Anyway, Clara and Warner live somewhere else. Christian and Victoria live in the house Christian had built for them and," he blew out a breath. "I'm back as the resident of the house."

"It sounds like a magical place."

"Magical?"

She nodded. "Your parents met and married. Your aunt married the man living in the house. Your sister is married. Your cousins are married." She turned her head toward him. "Your uncle. Did he remarry?"

Tyler chuckled. "Yes. He remarried his ex-wife."

"Magical," she sighed.

He'd never thought about it that way, but she was right. Now he lived there and here was this amazing woman.

Tyler shifted from his position on the boulder and slid down until his feet hit the water. "Oh! We've been up there longer than I thought."

He reached for Courtney's hand and eased her down. "It is a bit colder, isn't it?" She gasped as her feet hit the water.

Tyler steadied her with his hands on her hips. As though instinct kicked in, she reached for his arms and then slid her hands up to his shoulders.

"Thank you for sharing your spot with me," she said with her voice light.

"My pleasure."

He took her hand and led her out of the creek.

COURTNEY WAS quiet in the car, but she was a sight sitting there in her bright yellow dress with a yellow rose tucked in her hair from his grandmother's rose garden. Tyler figured there was no harm in taking one since his grandmother had already left for the night.

As he neared the neighborhood Courtney directed him to, he shifted a look her way again. "Have you heard from your parents? Do you need to call them and let them know you're safe?"

"When they realize I'm gone, they'll call."

"It's been hours."

"I know." She rested her head back against the seat.

Tyler knew that if his mother had known how to reach him while he was gone, she'd have called multiple times a day. His father would have as well. Oh, who was he kidding? Every member of his family would call him. It had only been Spencer whom he kept in touch with, and that was briefly too.

He turned down the street as she'd directed him, and slowed.

"Fourth house on the left," she said.

He looked for the numbers she'd given him. "You live here?" he asked looking at the house that nearly mirrored his own.

"Yes. For now I do."

"I live six blocks away."

She turned to him now with a smile. "You're near." Her voice had lifted.

"I am. I can't believe we live this close to each other."

"Fate, Tyler."

"I'm beginning to believe it."

Tyler pulled up in front of the house and put the car in park. "I'll walk you up," he said just as her cell phone rang with a song he wasn't familiar with.

"It's my mother. She noticed."

"I can wait."

She shook her head. "No, I'll let myself in." Courtney leaned across the car and held her hand out until she found his face. While her phone still rang, she pulled him toward her and pressed a kiss to his lips. "Thank you for saving me today."

As she eased back, she pressed the button on her phone and raised it to her ear. She didn't say anything, but Tyler could hear her mother's voice on the other end. As she climbed out, he could hear her say, "Yes, Mother. I know, Mother."

He wanted to walk her up, but she seemed just fine. From the back of the little purse she'd carried at the funeral, she pulled her cane out and walked up the front steps as he figured she'd done a million times before.

With her cane tucked under her arm, she searched for her keys. Sliding them into the door, and pushing it open, she disappeared into the dark house.

Out of instinct he waited for lights to turn on, but they never did. No, Courtney Field didn't need lights to see the world, he thought as he put the car into drive. She saw more than anyone he'd ever known—himself included.

CHAPTER 14

The rose was still fragrant and Courtney rolled the stem between her fingers, under her nose. Tyler had made one of the worst days of her life tolerable.

Her mother, on the other hand, had easily solidified it back to one of the worst with one phone call. It had taken them nearly three hours to notice she'd left.

Her mother hadn't asked if Courtney was okay. She hadn't even asked where she was. She'd led in with, "Did you leave the house?" and, "You were supposed to be my support."

Courtney couldn't help but wonder, if she was supposed to have supported her, how was it that it had taken her mother so long to realize Courtney wasn't even there?

As she'd assumed, her mother said she'd be over the next morning at nine to go through Fitz's things. Courtney would have liked to have held off just a bit. There were items she'd like to keep. Things that meant something to her and her mother would never know. This was one of those times when her sight hindered her from just doing what she wanted. She couldn't see those items.

Courtney leaned toward her nightstand and pressed the

button on her clock. It told her it was eleven o'clock at night. She'd managed to wallow in the house, alone, for hours. Her mind buzzed with thoughts of her mother arriving in ten hours.

Reaching toward her nightstand again, Courtney picked up her phone and held it in her hands. There were friends not too far away, they'd come over if she asked, right? But at that moment she couldn't think of one that she'd want to be with. Cousins? No. She didn't even have any of those.

There was only one choice.

TYLER PROCESSED THE NOISE. That was his phone ringing on his dresser. What the hell time was it?

He kicked off the sheet and got to his feet. Shuffling through the room with his eyes closed he found his phone on what he knew would be the last ring.

"Yeah?" His voice cracked as he'd said it.

"Oh, I woke you. Tyler, I'm so sorry. I'll talk to you..."

"Courtney?" His eyes were fully open now.

"Yes. I'm sorry."

He scrubbed his hand over his face. "No. Don't be sorry. What time is it?"

"It's eleven."

"Eleven? Geeze, I'm becoming an old man. I've been asleep for hours. I guess today wore me out." He walked to the bed and sat down on the end of it. "Is everything okay?"

She didn't answer right away and that worried him.

"Everything is fine. I really shouldn't have called."

"I think I told you on the plane to call anytime."

She let out a weak laugh. "You did." He heard her suck in a breath. "Okay, the reason I'm calling is that I want to go through my brother's things."

Tyler wanted to laugh but he forced it back. This wasn't the time. "Didn't you say you thought your mother would want to do that?"

"Yes. And she'll be here at nine in the morning."

"You did say she'd do that."

"But there are things I want to keep. Parts of him she will box up and I'll never find them. But, Tyler, I need a set of seeing eyes. I can't find the items I want."

"You need help before she gets there?"

"Yes."

"I'll be over in a half hour."

THE DOORBELL RANG EXACTLY a half hour after Courtney had called. He'd come. He'd said he would and he had.

Courtney walked to the door. "Tyler?"

"Yes, it's me," he said from the other side of the door.

She pulled it open. "Thank you for coming."

"My pleasure."

"Come in." She stepped back and felt him brush by her as he walked through the door. "I'll try to not keep you long. I just need to do this for my own peace of mind."

"I understand." Courtney felt his fingers take her hand and give it a squeeze. "Do you mind if I turn a few lights on?"

She laughed. "Of course. Fitz used to say the same thing. He was forever bumping into things. Nothing in this house ever moved, but he could run into it."

Courtney heard the click of the lamp on the end table and could see the adjustment in light.

"Thanks. Okay, what do we need to do?" he asked.

"Right. Let's get started. You'll need to be getting back to bed. I shouldn't have awakened you. It was selfish of me and…"

He'd moved to her and his hands were on her hips. She could feel his breath on her cheek and then his lips pressed against hers.

Tyler's lips were soft and his mouth tasted of mint. He'd brushed his teeth before he'd come and she found it endearing. Perhaps he'd wanted to come. Perhaps he'd had plans to kiss her, too.

What was she doing letting him kiss her? Her brother had died and she'd buried him. He was here to help her. And—as her parents would see it—he was a stranger.

But as she lifted her arms around his neck and he deepened the kiss, she found she didn't care.

Courtney had met him only days ago on a flight that was a mere few hours. But she'd spent nearly the whole day with him today and he'd kissed her over and over. What did it mean when in such a short time she was so comfortable around him?

This had never happened to her before. And though she enjoyed the game of trying to get the attention of men by dropping her scarf, she'd never caught one.

CHAPTER 15

$\mathcal{T}$yler eased back from their kiss. "I shouldn't do that to you," he said as he pressed his forehead to hers.

"Why?"

"I just met you. You have a lot going on in your life and I'm trying to put mine back together."

"All the more reason I think we should kiss and enjoy each other. We both need someone."

"But when the need is gone..."

"It'll never be gone. There's an acceptance going on here. You're trying to accept what you didn't know, and I'm trying to accept what I'll never get back—my brother."

Tyler took her hands and linked their fingers. "I didn't expect this when I met you on the plane."

"How could you have?"

"Did you?"

Courtney shook her head. "No, you just smelled good."

That made him chuckle. "Thank you for calling me."

"I couldn't think of anyone else I wanted to have over to help me with this."

Tyler released her hand and stroked his down her hair. "I

know this is all new. You don't know me from Adam, but you saying that means a great deal. I'm never going to let you down on purpose, Courtney. I can't guarantee I won't fail you at some point. But it won't be on purpose."

She tucked her lips in between her teeth and let his words resonate. "So, if you disappear from me it won't be on purpose?"

There was no way to keep her words controlled. They shook on her voice like a wave of panic for the ears to hear.

"I'm saying I'm not perfect."

"I'd despise you if you were."

"I've broken the heart of everyone I love. I walked away when they all needed me."

"But you came back."

"I never should have gone."

For a moment she had to remind herself that they were both momentarily broken. As much of a pillar of strength as he'd been all day, his involvement with her was stirring up feelings in him he hadn't yet dealt with. Fair enough. She'd called him in the middle of the night to help her deal with her feelings. She could certainly allow him a moment of pity.

"Three years in the life of a man is not that long, Tyler. In a few months the pain you think you caused will not be relevant. In a year it'll be a slight sting. In three more years—nearly forgotten."

"You don't understand. I come from this perfect family and I'm not perfect."

"Again, I'd despise you if you were. I cannot imagine your family is perfect. No family is perfect."

"Mine is," he said very matter-of-fact.

"What a compliment to them that you think so. But I can guarantee you they aren't."

He cupped her face in his hands. "Sunday. Dinner. Are you up for a crazy night?"

She raised her hands to his wrists. "What does that have to do with your family?"

"Everything. I want you to meet perfection."

Courtney swallowed back the tears—the excitement—the fear. "You want me to meet your family?"

"A woman who drops her scarf for a good smelling man to pick up and spends the worst day of her life kissing that man shouldn't be afraid of one dinner with his family."

"Right. I'm not afraid. I'll meet your family."

He stepped in and brushed a kiss on her lips. "I should warn you that…"

Courtney lifted her fingers to his lips. "Don't warn me. You'll just get me worked up if I think there is something that is going to happen. I'll be fine. You met my family and survived."

He chuckled as she pulled her fingers back. "I'm thinking I'll need to meet them again. Our introduction wasn't one of great timing, and when they realize you spent the day with me and not at their house, they'll probably change their mind about me."

"No they won't," she quickly answered. She wasn't about to let her parents turn on Tyler. He'd been nothing but gracious. And they weren't the only ones who lost Fitz. She'd lost him and she would mourn and hurt much longer than either of them she was sure. If she needed Tyler in her life then she'd have him.

Courtney stepped back. "C'mon, let's go upstairs and find those items I wanted."

She held out her hand for the handrail that should be within a few feet of her. When her hand came to the newel post, she began her way up the stairs.

"Just turn on whatever lights you need to. I'm a tad bit oblivious to its need," she said and he chuckled from behind her.

At the sixteenth step, which she'd counted a million times, she turned left down the hallway to Fitz's room. With her hand on the wall she felt for the door, turned the knob, and pushed it open.

Courtney stepped in and heard the switch of the light as Tyler stepped in behind her.

"Baseball player, huh?"

"Yes. A good one too."

"I can see that. There has to be fifteen trophies in here alone."

She nodded and stepped in further feeling her brother surrounding her as she did.

"He held the record for home runs during high school."

"Impressive. My cousin was a semi-professional ball player. His room didn't look much different."

"Which cousin?"

"Christian, Christian Keller."

She turned her head toward him. "Pitcher."

Now he laughed hard. "You know who Christian Keller is?"

"Because of Fitz. We used to go to the games." She couldn't believe the connection. "You have quite an impressive family tree. A baseball player, a country music artist, an oil heiress, and you... heir to Benson, Benson, and Hart."

The air in the room grew thick and Courtney knew she'd crossed the line. But she waited for him to make a comment. The pain of the passing moments before he spoke was agonizing.

"I guess you've done some research, huh?"

Courtney let her shoulders drop. "I'm sorry. I hope you understand my unique position. I needed to know who it was that comforted me so much that day."

"I understand it, heir to the Fitzpatrick Financial Corporation."

Courtney bit the inside of her cheek. "You did your research too."

"Easily done."

She nodded in agreement. "My father is afraid you might be a gold digger."

"Couldn't care less about someone's money. I don't care about what is in someone's bank account. I've met men who are billionaires and they don't have a bit of emotional worth to them. Thanks to my oil heiress aunt," he emphasized and she felt the words squeeze at her, "I've met women who lived on the streets with their children begging for food. They asked for help and they now help others. They have jobs—careers. They're wealthier than any man with a million dollars."

She wondered if it was possible to feel love at first sight—even when the physical sight was impaired. If it was possible—and again she wasn't sure it was—she was sure she'd just stumbled into it. Tyler Benson was nearly too good to be true.

*a*dmittedly, going through someone's personal belongings, especially when you didn't know them, was a little nerve wracking, Tyler thought. But for Courtney, he was pretty sure he'd do damn near anything.

He couldn't pinpoint exactly what it was about this woman, as he opened her brother's dresser drawers in search of a box, that would make him drive over in the middle of the night just because she'd asked.

Really he'd never done so much for any other woman before, and he'd just met Courtney.

"I found a box. Black with a Marine sticker on it."

"Yes!" she shouted and stood from her seat on the bed.

He placed the box in her hands and she ran her fingers over the edge of the sticker. When she opened it there was a gold Rolex watch inside. She pulled it out and handed it to him.

"Read the inscription please."

Tyler took the watch and turned it over. "To Fitz. It's your time. Love Court."

He watched her body relax as she smiled. "That's the one. I want that in my possession."

Tyler handed her the watch and she placed it back in the box.

"He called you Court?"

"Yes. He was the only one allowed to. I hate it, but not when he said it."

"It's a beautiful watch," Tyler added as he pushed the drawer, in which he'd found the box, back into place.

"I bought it for him when he joined the Marines. I'd been very mad at him over that. His enlisting was my father's idea, not his. He didn't seem to mind, but I was pissed. We argued from the time he graduated until he was ready to go to boot camp. I gave it to him before he left because by then I'd realized it was his time to leave me and go into the world. He'd been protecting me and sheltering me for his entire life. It was time for him to go change the world."

She ran her hand over the top of the box. "I guess the world changed him."

Tyler watched her for a moment. "What else can I help you find?"

Courtney turned and set the watch on the bed.

They spent an hour in the room finding small items that Courtney didn't want boxed up and stored for the rest of eternity. The watch, a jacket, a baseball, and a notebook were all they took out of the room. When they were done, Courtney closed the bedroom door.

"I'm going to put these away in my room. I'll meet you downstairs in a few minutes," she said as she passed him and walked into the room down the hall.

Tyler walked downstairs and waited. Just as promised, she returned a few minutes later.

"I suppose I should go now. If you need anything else, just call."

Courtney reached for him and he took her hand. "Would you stay? I mean, just for a little bit. I know it's past midnight, but..."

"I'll stay."

"I could use the company. I don't mean we'd do anything but sit on the couch and watch TV, but…"

He gave her hand a squeeze. "I said I'd stay."

Courtney walked to the TV, turned it on, and handed Tyler the remote. "I'm going to make some tea to relax. Would you like some?"

"That would be nice."

"You find something to watch. I'll be right back."

He sat down and watched her from the couch. Everything in the small kitchen was in an appointed place and she moved with ease through the room as she filled the water, set it on the stove to boil, and pulled down two mugs.

There was a gracefulness to her—a peace. He needed that kind of peace in his life too. Tomorrow—or in a few hours—he'd meet his father in his office downtown and they'd discuss Tyler's future at Benson, Benson, and Hart.

In a few years, his father would want to retire. His cousin Ed was holding the reins now, but Ed had always known that the company would eventually be Tyler and Spencer's. But Tyler wasn't sure he was cut out for real estate development on such a grand scale.

Spencer had a mind for business. Tyler wasn't even sure what he had a mind for. He'd made due for three years. He'd learned a lot about the world, about making ends meet, and about himself. Yeah, he'd learned that he was selfish and self-centered.

Tyler let out a breath. He didn't want to be that person anymore.

The kettle on the stove snapped him from his thoughts. Tyler stood and walked to the kitchen as she lifted the kettle from the stove.

"I'll try to stay out of your way," he said leaning up against the counter.

"Fitz used to say that too." She held a mug steady with her hand, rested the spout of the kettle on the mug, and poured. "I don't really know why I'll miss him so much around here. His things were here, but he wasn't here more than a few weeks a year."

"You gave him a place to call home."

She shook her head and replaced the kettle on the stove. "No, he did that for me. He didn't want me living under my parents' feet for the rest of my life. So he bought this place and moved me in. It's been my refuge."

Tyler assumed that was a good use of the wealth he assumed Courtney and Fitz had at such young ages.

"You were close, you and your brother."

"Very close," she admitted. "He felt responsible for me—for my situation." She handed him a mug. "There are tea bags in the container on the table. You can choose what kind you want."

Tyler picked up his mug and walked toward the table. He waited for her to set her mug down and take a seat, and then he sat next to her.

As he chose a tea, none of which were full strength coffee flavor, he asked, "Why did he feel responsible for your situation?"

Courtney opened her tea bag and bobbed it in her mug. "Because I've been blind since I was eight."

"Right."

She tucked her hair behind her ears and then cupped the mug in her hands. "Because he was the one who scared the horse who kicked me and eventually that caused me to lose my sight."

CHAPTER 17

There hadn't been any kind of auditory gasp or movement, but Courtney knew the silence of shock too.

Tyler's tea bag bobbed against his mug as he lifted it in and out in a nervous ritual. He drummed his fingers against his thigh. She could almost hear his brain turning, trying to think of something clever like everyone else had when she'd told them.

"How old was Fitz when that happened?"

Tyler had lived up to his element of surprise. He didn't coddle the fact that an accident by her little brother at such a young age had robbed her of what everyone considered normal.

"Four."

"That must have really affected him."

"It did. He didn't talk to me for a long time. He was afraid of me. By the time he was nine he was getting in fights over me. Then he was protecting me." She pulled the bag of tea out of her mug and set it on a napkin she had pulled from the holder on the table. "He challenged me. He pushed me. But he always had my back. Like this house. He bought it a year ago."

"So when he was nineteen?"

"Yes. It pissed my father off too. He took the money from his trust fund and bought a house."

"That's a sturdy financial decision."

She laughed. "It was. He put my name on the title too so no one could ever take it away from me."

Courtney heard him lean in and rest his arms on the table. "Do you ever think he knew he wouldn't come back?"

In a nervous habit, she tucked her hair back again. "He was very insightful like that. He'd never have told me though. He knew I was worried enough."

Tyler covered her hand with his. "I think it sounds like you two made quite a pair."

She smiled. "We did. I'm going to miss him so much I don't even know how I'm going to deal with that." That pain was creeping into her chest—the kind of pain that started as an ache and quickly began to choke you. Tears burned her throat and her breath began to hold in her lungs.

"You won't do it alone. I'll be here."

She nodded. It was all she could do. He would be there. He'd said it more than once, and she believed he meant it.

TEA HAD TURNED into a long talk about the man that Fitz was. They'd moved from the kitchen to the couch, and when Tyler's phone rang, that was what had awakened him.

He shifted on the couch. His arm was numb from having had it draped over Courtney for the past few hours.

The ringing had her stirring too. She sat up and rubbed her face.

"What is that? Mine or yours?" Her voice shook with sleep.

"Mine." He looked at the screen. "It's my brother. Hey, Spence," he said trying to make his eyes focus on the light coming in from the window.

"Want a ride? I'm heading into town. I can swing by and pick you up," Spencer asked.

"A ride? What the hell time is it?"

His brother laughed. "Man, it's a quarter till nine. I told Dad you'd be there by nine-thirty."

"Crap!" He stood from the couch. "I'll be there closer to ten. But I can drive in. Do me a favor, have them get me a parking space and I'll take the elevator up to his office."

"You still have the key?"

"Yeah, just tell him I'll be there."

"I will. Where are you?" His brother's tone had that edge to it —the kind that teetered on laughter.

"Bite me," he said as Spencer started to laugh. He pushed the button to hang up the call as Courtney stood next to him.

"What time is it?"

"Eight forty-five."

"Oh, God! My mother will be here any minute. You have to get out of here."

"I'm gone." He hurried to the front door with Courtney holding his hand. "I'm sorry. I didn't mean to fall asleep."

"Oh, it's my fault. I called you here and then kept you here."

Tyler searched his pocket for his keys and pulled them out. "I'll talk to you later." He bent down and pressed a kiss to her lips which must have surprised her.

He opened the door and hurried to his car. This wasn't quite the way he'd wanted to prove to his father that he was man enough to accept responsibilities.

As he drove away from Courtney's house, he passed a black Mercedes. The driver slowed, but Tyler pressed on toward home. He needed to take a shower and get to his father. The bonus to it all would be that in a few hours he could call Courtney and compare their day.

Tyler turned on his signal at the stop sign, looked both ways, and turned with a smile. He couldn't believe how much he looked forward to that call.

CHAPTER 18

*T*he front door opened, and Courtney could hear her mother's shoes on the hardwood floor.

"Courtney, where are you? Are you okay? Are you here? Where are you?"

Courtney let out a groan. "Mother, I'm upstairs. I'll be right down."

She heard the familiar thud of her mother's purse landing on the coffee table and then the coffee pot being filled at the sink. If it was past two in the afternoon, she would have heard the sound of the cupboard where the wine was kept being opened.

Courtney brushed through her hair and fastened it atop her head in a ponytail. She'd changed her clothes quickly and would have to remember later to pick the others up off the floor or she'd trip over them. But for now, she was in a hurry to get downstairs.

Her mother was pacing the kitchen when she'd made her way down to her. She could hear the click-clack of her mother's expensive Italian shoes on the tile. They made a different sound than heavier soled ones.

"Good morning, Mother."

"Don't good morning me," her mother said and her voice shook. "I saw him. I saw him drive away from here."

Courtney walked to the counter and took a mug down from the cupboard. "And who did you see?"

"That man you left the funeral with yesterday. You left me there alone."

"You said it was okay to go with him."

"To our house. You left."

Courtney poured herself a cup of coffee, and when it warmed her body, she realized just how tired she was. She and Tyler must have only rested a few hours.

"I couldn't stand to be there any longer. We said goodbye to Fitz. I listened to everyone mumble about how sad it was. He was too young. He was a good solider. You would miss him, but it was a sacrifice for the country." She was gripping the mug now. "And I was tired of hearing the whispers about how well I was doing despite my short comings."

"No one said that," her mother argued.

"I heard them, Mother. I can't see them hide their lips behind their hands. I hear their petty little voices."

She could hear her mother sip her coffee and then set the mug on the table. "I just think it was inconsiderate of you to leave with a man during the reception. Do you know how that looks?"

"Like I needed some space? My brother was buried yesterday. My only brother."

Her mother clucked her tongue. "You'll need to move back home."

Courtney set her mug on the counter and fisted her hands on her hips. "I am almost twenty-five years old. I will be just fine here."

"Don't be ridiculous. Without Fitz here…"

"Mother, Fitz was never here. He probably slept in that bed twenty times in the last year. I've lived here, by myself, all that time."

Her mother's fingers drummed on the table. "And now you have men staying here."

Courtney grit her teeth together. "That's not what happened."

"That's how it looked. And you should see you. Your shirt is on backward."

She hated when her mother said it like that instead of nicely telling her. It didn't happen often, but she'd been in a hurry.

Courtney picked up her coffee and walked to the table where she sat down across from her mother.

"Tyler was kind enough to drive me home after we took a drive."

"A drive. You let a man you don't know just drive you around?"

Courtney let the smile settle on her lips and she was sure it would drive her mother mad. "He took me to his grandmother's house and introduced me to her."

She could feel the tension begin to dissolve. "He took you to meet his grandmother?"

"Yes. She doesn't live far from you. Audrey Benson. She's a very nice woman. We had iced tea on her patio, walked through her rose garden, and went to the stables to meet the horses."

That made her mother tense. "I don't like you around horses. You know that."

"One mistake. One misfortune. I'm not going to deny myself the pleasures of horses."

"Courtney," her mother's voice went soft. "Aren't you afraid?"

"Of horses? No."

"Of anything?"

The only thing Courtney was afraid of was becoming petty like her mother. That wasn't even fair, she thought as she took a sip of her coffee. Her mother was a kind woman who just needed a lot of attention. Fitz would give that to her. Her father would play it off as a disease. And her mother would fuss over Courtney when it suited her so that Courtney would give her attention. Other than that, no, Courtney wasn't afraid of anything.

"It's a waste of time to be afraid of anything. You have to look at the world each morning and realize it's a wonder to just have another day."

Her mother reached across the table and took her hand. "I forget you were born with the overly optimistic gene."

"Good thing I was. And, Mother, I'm very optimistic about Tyler Benson."

Her mother tugged her hand back. "I was afraid of that."

TYLER PULLED into the parking space his brother had left for him. He turned off the car, made sure he had his elevator key, and climbed out. The elevator went straight to his father's office. It was certainly a perk when you owned the entire building, he thought.

Normally, he wouldn't use the entrance. He wasn't so good that he couldn't walk through the front doors, but he was running late, he looked like hell, and man he was hungry.

When the elevator door opened, he stepped out into his father's corner office. It was no surprise there were three smiling faces there to greet him. His father, his brother, and his cousin Ed.

"I owe you five bucks," Ed said to Spencer. "He did show up."

Tyler let his shoulders drop. "And you're all sitting here waiting to see if I'd run, huh?"

"Your reputation precedes you now," Ed moved toward him and placed his hand on his shoulder. "But it's good to have you here."

"Thanks."

His father, who was leaned up against his desk, stood and looked at him. He'd heard it his whole life, "You look just like your father." Looking at him now, he realized that in forty some years, he'd be just as distinguished. At sixty-four, his father was a fit and handsome man. And, from the photographs Tyler had seen, Zach Benson looked just like his father Tyler Benson, whom Tyler was named for.

"Why don't you two give me and Tyler a few minutes together?" his father said.

"Sure," Spencer agreed. "Just don't promote him to C.E.O. There is a whole initiation that has to happen. We don't have his underwear to hang from the flag pole yet."

Spencer and Ed chuckled as they walked toward the door. "Is hazing still out?" Ed asked as they walked out of the office.

"They're going to give you a hard time, but they're glad you're home," his father said.

"I don't know that I belong here." The words had come quickly and they weren't meant to hurt, but he'd seen his father's posture stiffen.

Zach Benson could keep his cool, and he did. He'd only nodded, smiled, and then led Tyler to the couch in the office to sit.

"If your mother heard you say you don't belong here, it would break her heart."

"Dad, I mean in the company. I know I belong in Nashville."

His father's shoulders softened and he relaxed back against the couch. "Now we're making progress. What are your hesitations about being part of BBH?"

Where did he start? He didn't like nepotism. He didn't like big corporations. He'd seen enough poverty over the past three years, he figured there had to be something he could do to change the world. The list went on and on.

"I don't think it's any secret that Spencer is cut out for all of this, just as Ed was. I'm not, Dad."

"You can learn."

Tyler nodded. "Yes. I could learn. But I think I could change the world if I tried. I think that Aunt Simone's charity work is more my style."

His father stretched his arm over the back of the couch and looked at him. "I never would have thought that would be her calling. But it was."

"She's changed a lot of lives."

"She has. Hers included."

Tyler had heard all the stories of his father and his aunt growing up together in France. His aunt still admitted that until she'd fallen in love with his Uncle Curtis, she'd had a crush on his father. It all seemed weird to him, but his Aunt Simone wasn't the same woman then that she was now.

She was a strong figure in the community. She'd walked away from fortune and family to marry the man she truly loved. That did say a lot about her character.

Zach patted Tyler's thigh. "Are you thinking you'd like to talk to her about a job?"

Tyler shrugged. "I don't know the first thing about how to help people either. I don't know much about anything."

A smile formed on his father's lips. "You're selling yourself short."

"In the past three years I've held four jobs."

"Yes, and one of them was on a Pierpont Oil rig."

"You've talked to Uncle John?"

"We're a tight family."

He knew that. Wasn't that the part that drove him home —family?

"Tyler, I want you to do what you want to do. I will always have opportunity for you here. That's what fathers are for."

"Spencer and Ed belong here."

Zach nodded. "They do. Ed has always had it in him, and Spencer was designing things from the time he could put Legos together. You've always had your head somewhere else, and that's okay." Zach stood and Tyler followed. "Why don't you talk to

Simone? Feel out what you want to do. If you need something in the mean time, I could get you a job at the Starbucks downstairs."

That made Tyler laugh. "I'd rather work in the building permits department."

Zach rested his hand on Tyler's shoulder. "You give me the word and you'll have a position."

"I'll let you know," he said, but he was sure that working in an office that overlooked Nashville would make him crazy. Of course, the very fact that he was standing there in his father's office had Courtney crossing his mind, and it made him equally as uncomfortable.

He'd seen her mother pass by him. Surely Courtney was going through her own hell. Tonight. He'd call her tonight and they could compare horror stories. Corporate jobs verses meddling mothers. The thought nearly made him laugh.

First he'd head over to see his aunt. Suddenly helping the less fortunate seemed a lot more appealing than private elevators and parking spaces.

CHAPTER 19

*S*imone Keller's office was simple, and smaller than the room Tyler had occupied on the Pierpont Oil rig. She sat at her desk, pinched against the wall in the small medical clinic where she'd once worked, and now where she ran her charity. Her long black hair hung over her shoulder. Tyler could hear her, and he knew that a phone receiver was pressed to her ear under that curtain of hair.

As she spoke about a fundraising event, she looked up at the doorway to see him standing there. A smile lifted her cheeks and sparkled in her eyes.

"That sounds great. If we can get them to help us financially, we'll gain a lot more followers and revenue." She nodded and took a few notes on a pad in front of her. "Okay. Let me know what you find out."

She hung up the phone and stood. The chair in her office hit the wall behind her and she shimmied out from behind the desk and moved directly to him.

"To what do I owe this pleasure?" Her French accent was still deep, even after all the years she'd lived in Tennessee.

"I'm out visiting. I just left Dad's office."

"He did say you were going to stop by there today. So what is your new title? What kind of view does your office have?"

Tyler rubbed his hand over the back of his neck. "I didn't take a job yet. I'm not sure commercial real estate development is my thing."

She nodded. "I once used to travel the world attending meetings and listening to men discuss oil. It didn't seem to be for me either."

"I think your work here is more important."

She smiled wide and pride in what she did was evident. "I received a phone call today from a young mother who has relocated in Ohio. Her daughter, who had been sexually abused by the mother's boyfriend, is in school and doing wonderfully. And the mother has a good job and just got a promotion. She called to thank me. Isn't that wonderful?"

And it was the look on his aunt's face that told him he couldn't thrive in corporate America, even if his name was on the side of the building.

"You know, Tyler, I did not know this would have been my calling. One day I did something that changed someone's life, and it changed my life too. I'm sure your father would agree that he didn't expect me to create something so selflessly."

He didn't know about that, but then again he'd only ever known Simone as a woman who gave her all to help others.

"Anyway," she went on, "why are you here?"

"I was thinking maybe this was more my speed. I thought I'd see if your organization was in need of someone who knew nothing at all."

She laughed easily, crossed her arms in front of her, and studied him. "You want to work within my organization?"

"I know you probably don't have the funding for very many employees. My rent is low. I'm bumming a car from my parents. And I really don't want to work in construction."

She nodded and pressed her painted lips together. "I have a

gala coming up in three months. It is one of my biggest events of the year and nets the organization most of its operating costs. Are you up to the challenge of helping to organize it?"

"Really? I'd love to try."

She nodded and held out her dainty, well manicured hand to shake his. "Well, Mr. Tyler Benson, I would love to work with you. And I am not a very nice boss."

That caused him to laugh as he leaned in and kissed his aunt on the cheek. "I won't let you down."

"I know. If you do you will see that not so nice side of me." She stepped back toward her desk. "Avery is helping put the gala together. Perhaps the two of you should get together and begin to make plans."

"Is she going to be upset to have me helping her?"

Simone sat down behind her desk. "Do you want to work for your father?"

Tyler cringed. "No. Not really."

"Avery feels much the same way. And since she has no interest in medicine either, she will not be following in her father's footsteps. I think she will be happy you came back."

"Thank you."

"No, thank you. I think you will do very well here."

CHAPTER 20

*S*itting in Fitz's bedroom with her mother was nearly as excruciating as Fitz's funeral the day before, Courtney thought. Her mother had picked up nearly every item in his room and cried over it. She'd brought boxes and loaded them. Each box was labeled, and Courtney added a braille label as well. Her mother had said that the attic in the garage would be where the boxes would be stored, and it would make sense if Courtney could identify the boxes.

Courtney didn't understand the rush to get his items packed away. Wouldn't it be okay to keep him around just a little longer? Wasn't it bad enough he was gone for good? Did they have to hide him too?

She kept her calm knowing she'd taken the items she'd wanted. Tyler had helped her there. He'd been helping her quite a bit.

Did he understand that his kindness on the plane had helped her accept the mission she'd undertaken of escorting her brother home? Having him at the funeral had made it tolerable. Tyler had let her escape, he'd let her cry, he'd come when she called. How was it a man she'd known a week could change her life?

"I have a few more boxes in the car. I'll be right back," her mother said and Courtney heard her leave the room.

Courtney laid back on her brother's bed and let out a long breath. Was her mother right? Would the pain be less if all of his things were tucked away? Or would it hurt more to know that the room would be empty and he'd be gone—all of him?

"Courtney!" Her mother's voice rang down the hall forcing her to sit up and then rise to her feet. "Courtney!"

She followed her mother's voice to her own bedroom.

"Mother, what is it?"

"What did you do? What did you and that man do?"

Her mother's voice shook and she could hear the tears being sucked back.

"I have no idea what you're talking about."

"Your clothes are piled in the floor. You never scatter your things around. Courtney, you don't know him."

She could feel the heat rise in her cheeks. Her heart rate kicked up to match the racing blood that coursed through her system.

"I can't believe you can't accept my word that nothing happened. I was in a hurry. I changed quickly."

"He spent the night?"

"Mother, I'm nearly twenty-five years old. If I wanted a man to spend the night in my bedroom, in my house, I damn well better be able to do so. You have no room to discuss this with me."

"Don't talk to me like that."

"Why? Because you forgot that you had me at sixteen? You forgot that I don't know my birth father?" The anger was fresh now. She wasn't quite done. "If I had wanted Tyler Benson to share my bed, then damn it, he'd have shared it."

"Don't talk like that," her mother scolded.

"I'll talk the way I want. I am an adult. I am tired of you

treating me like a little girl who can't do anything for herself. Fitz believed in me. Why can't you?"

"You're disabled. You need me."

That was the breaking point. She knew that her mother was lucky she was disabled or she would find out just how much anger she'd stored her entire life. But she still had her words and she wasn't done using them yet.

"I'd like to have you know that I can do anything. I've been told I see things those of you who have sight can't see. Mother, I'm not the disabled one. You are. You're emotionally disabled. I am perfectly capable of having a life and loving a man."

"You love this man?"

"Is that all you've heard?" She lifted her hands in the air. "Maybe you'd better go."

She'd never wanted to be alone so much in her life. It had been a good ten years since she'd mentioned her birth and paternity to her mother. But it was the one button she could push with her mother. It was proof that everyone, even her mother, made judgment calls that cost them something dearly.

Courtney had never held her mother's decisions against her—unless it benefited her in an argument like the one they were having. She'd only been three when the only father she'd ever known came into her life. Fitz was born just shy of her mother's twenty-first birthday. Duane Field gave them stability. They traveled the world, the family of a soldier. He taught Courtney discipline. He gave her a name. He loved her mother, and that was the most important thing—and he loved Courtney too.

He'd been known to stand up for Courtney when her mother's emotional stability challenged her daughter. For the first year, when Courtney was learning to live without her sight, her mother cried nearly everyday. But Courtney had heard her in one of her meltdowns. She regretted having a daughter that wasn't normal anymore.

Only her father understood her mother enough that he knew

she hadn't meant it. Even Courtney knew she didn't mean it. When Mary Field couldn't control a situation, words flew that she'd later beg to have taken back. Courtney was sure this would be one of those times. But for now she wanted her mother to leave.

She could hear her mother's breath quicken. "Courtney, I don't want you making decisions you can't take back. I mean—I think you'd better…"

"Mother, I'm a grown up who understands my situation. I'm a blind woman. Fine, that's not a problem really. But I understand the challenge. You had two kids living in Germany by the time you were my age. We all have challenges."

"I don't want to see you struggle."

If that was what she was trying to protect her from, Mary Field was failing miserably.

"Mother, my only struggle is trying to keep my calm right now. Tomorrow it will be dealing with the fact that Fitz won't be emailing me. The day after that, it will be knowing he's not coming back—ever. And the next day will be the same. And the day after that. The difference will be, I'll still be blind. You can't protect me from that. And if—if—I choose to have an adult relationship with Tyler then I will. But that has nothing to do with you."

"Come home with me," her mother pleaded.

"No. I live here. I have lived here for a year." She held her arms out until her mother took her hands and Courtney pulled her in. "Mother, he's gone. We have to wake up tomorrow and keep living. We can't spend the rest of our lives blaming each other."

Her mother sobbed in Courtney's ear. "What will we do?"

"Live, Mother. He'd be very disappointed in us if we stopped living to mourn him."

"You're right." Her mother stepped back. "I'm sorry we said horrible things to each other."

Courtney was sure that was to even the playing field, though Courtney didn't regret anything she'd said.

"Go home, Mother. Take a long bath and rest."

"I will." She kissed Courtney on the cheek. "We can finish his room later."

Finally she was making sense.

Courtney listened as her mother walk down the steps and shut the front door. She felt the pain of the day drag through her and she sat in the floor and cried. She missed Fitz so much. She could convince her mother to go on and try to be the voice of reason, but in truth would Courtney ever accept the fate they'd all been handed?

CHAPTER 21

*T*yler's mind had buzzed since he'd left his aunt's office. He wanted to celebrate and cook dinner for Courtney. After all, one of his jobs had been as a sous-chef at a family restaurant for a few months. He could pull something together.

He'd arranged to meet with his cousin Avery tomorrow at lunch, and they could begin melding ideas for the gala his aunt would put on to raise money for her organization.

He was honored that Simone took him into consideration. He felt right about helping others.

Though his mind was filled with the possibilities ahead, Tyler smiled as he pushed his cart through the grocery store because Courtney was heavy on his mind. There was something in the way that she carried herself, the way she thought, just the way she lived that made Tyler envious. She had an acceptance about things that had had him driving over to his sister's house first thing the other night to apologize. And wasn't he glad he had. On Sunday he'd go back again, this time as an expected guest, though he'd believed that there had always been an extra seat there just in case he was to drop in. This time, however, he'd take Courtney with him.

The thought made him warm. He'd only known her a few days, but the woman had changed his life already. Just the vision she had, without physically seeing the world, made him see it more clearly.

Yes, she might have just made him accept everything that he thought was wrong with his life. Thank God, Courtney thought he smelled good enough to drop her scarf.

Tyler called her around one o'clock and invited her to dinner. He wasn't sure her voice was very uplifting, but she'd accepted his invitation and that, he thought, had made her sound a little happier.

Six o'clock just wasn't going to get there fast enough. He wanted to see her. Be with her. Oh, and the urge to kiss her was weighing big time on his mind.

TYLER PUT AWAY his groceries and looked up a recipe for something with chicken on the computer. If he'd done that first, he wouldn't just be putting in available ingredients in the search box. Maybe Clara or Avery knew a thing or two about cooking. It would be nice if he didn't have to think so hard each time he wanted to cook a meal for Courtney.

Tyler sat back in his chair and just looked at the computer screen. He did want to cook for Courtney. He realized, that even in the few brief times they'd spent together, he'd grown closer to her than he had anyone in years.

He smiled to himself. His mother and father were only together about a year before they married. Avery's parents had her before they got married. Clara ran off and married Warner in Vegas. Even Ed and Darcy fell in love right after meeting. Could that be what he was feeling? Were the feelings he was having for Courtney deeper than just this acceptance she made him feel?

Really, did it matter? He liked her. He liked her a lot. As long as they got along and wanted to be with each other, they could see where things went between them.

He let out a deep breath. There was something inside of him that made him think there just might be something between them.

⁓

At SIX O'CLOCK, Tyler rang the bell at Courtney's door. He stood there and wondered if she was even home. He was just about to ring it again when she opened the door.

"I was afraid you weren't home," he said.

She smiled easily at his voice. "I guess I fell asleep. I was a little tired after staying up all night and then putting up with my mother today."

"Is everything okay?"

"Do you have wine at your house?"

"Yes."

"Let's talk about it over wine." She smiled sweetly. "Let me get my purse."

Courtney stepped back into the house and a moment later came to the door with her purse on her shoulder. She shut the door, locked it, and then held out her hand to reach for his arm.

Tyler moved next to her, but she stopped from taking his arm, and instead rested her hand on his shoulder and turned him toward her.

Her other hand came up to his face and her thumb grazed over his lip. "You shaved."

"I did. The grizzly look is not good on me."

"I'll bet you're just as handsome either way."

"Thank you."

Courtney stepped in closer to him. "Would you mind if I test it out?"

"It?"

She laughed as she pulled his face closer to hers. "Your smooth cheek." She rested her cheek against his and his eyes drifted closed in anticipation. "Very nice."

Courtney's other hand came to his other cheek and she guided his lips to hers where she pressed a warm kiss to them. But she didn't back away. She stepped in until his only choice was to wrap his arms around her and hold her as much for balance as need to be near her.

Courtney opened her mouth to him and he took it. Her hands slid around his neck, and her fingers that entangled in his hair sent pulses of energy through his body.

As she eased back, he could still sense the tension in her. Her mother must have upset her quite a bit, not to mention he was sure she was beginning to miss her brother. That would only prove to grow deeper for a while, he assumed. He'd never lost anyone he was close to. His grandfather, whom he was named after, had passed years before he'd been born. But he remembered his mother talking about the depression his father had gone into.

Tyler could offer Courtney company and compassion. Surely that would be enough for now.

CHAPTER 22

*C*ourtney had longed for this moment since she'd awakened next to Tyler on the couch. Her mother's visit had put her in a less than sunny mood. She couldn't blame her mother for being the way she was, Courtney knew that. But she figured they'd butt heads a few more times before they'd each healed from Fitz's death.

Tyler was there now. She embraced the thought. He'd come to pick her up for dinner.

She took his arm and he led her to the curb where his car was parked.

"Where are you taking me?" She asked as she climbed into the car.

"Home."

Courtney hesitated for a moment. "Home?"

"I'm cooking for you."

A hundred different feelings burst inside of her like a bomb being detonated full of emotions.

"You're cooking me dinner?"

"I've been on the move for nearly three years. I haven't called anywhere home in that long either. I just feel like being home and cooking a decent meal—I hope. And being with a woman that fascinates me."

She could feel those doubtful emotions begin to fizzle out, and warmth began to surge through her. "I fascinate you?"

"In a million ways. Maybe I can share that with you tonight. I have a lot to talk about. I've had a wonderful day."

Tyler opened the car door and Courtney slid inside. She locked her seatbelt in place and Tyler closed the door. She wondered what had gone on in his day that could have made him so chipper. Hopefully she wouldn't dull his mood.

Tyler had the radio on, and it kicked into song when he started the car. Luke Bryan sang about playing a song again and again because a girl liked it. She was sure that if there was a song on the radio that would make her happy to hear over and over, Tyler would find it and play it until she'd had her fill.

The thought made her smile. What was it about this man who had been so lost that made her think he'd do something like that —for her?

As he drove, he reached for her hand and held it. She enjoyed this. Never in a million years would she have thought that a man would find her so interesting. And for some reason, she never thought he'd be sighted. She always figured the man she would get involved with would be blind too. After all, the only men she'd been with had been blind. There had been no driving around and holding hands. No searching through rooms for treasures. Oh, there had been the fumbling of clothes, buttons, and tripping over shoes—the memory had her stifling a laugh. But this was different.

She thought back to the boulder in the creek at his grandmother's, when she'd told him to close his eyes so he could see. It had awakened something in him. A sight.

She reminded herself that he was already healing when he got on that plane bound for Nashville. But she'd like to think in their few days together, she had helped him move closer to accepting who he was and how important his family was.

"So what made your day so good? Did you talk to your father about a job?"

He gave her hand a squeeze. "I did."

"When do you start?"

"Oh, I start tomorrow, but I'm not building anything."

Courtney turned her face toward him. "So you're in a different department?"

"I didn't take his job. I went looking for a different opportunity."

"Such as?"

"My first project, I guess, is as an event planner." He chuckled.

"Are you kidding me?"

"No. I went to my aunt and asked for a job."

"Your aunt. The one with the charity?"

"Yes. I have a need to do things for people who need it. I want to do something that will really matter in the long run."

"When did you decide on this?"

"When I was sitting in my father's office realizing that wasn't what I wanted."

She couldn't help but wonder if that was what fascinated him with her—was she someone he saw as a person who needed help?

There was nothing she thought was probably further from the truth, but the thought stuck for a moment.

"What kind of event planning will you be doing?" Courtney asked.

"I'm going to work with my cousin on putting together her fundraising gala. This one event nearly covers all her expenses."

Courtney felt him shift. "In fact, she said she had a call today from a woman whom she'd helped out. The daughter had been assaulted by the woman's boyfriend. But they had gotten away. She now had a good job and the girl was in school and doing well. I think this was exactly what she'd hoped for when she began her work."

"How did she get into this?"

"One day there was a woman who kept coming to the clinic. She had a baby with her, I think. But she was always beat up. My aunt, who had managed to get a job at the clinic, had given the woman the diamond earrings right out of her ears. Simone's father had bought them for her. It was enough for the woman to pawn to buy food, diapers, and get away from the man. The woman did just that, and in time she had a job, a new home, and a future. She worked with my aunt and the charity for years."

"She doesn't work for her anymore?"

"No. If I remember correctly she's some city council woman or something. What my aunt did for her changed her life and my aunt's. And when my aunt saw what one gesture like that could do, she knew she could help many more women and families."

Courtney couldn't wait to meet this aunt. She sounded amazing.

"So does she have some big office? What is the overhead like on something like that?"

He laughed again. "No. She certainly doesn't have a big office. In fact, she still works out of the clinic where she worked all those years ago. Her office hardly has room for her to turn around in. She could have had a nice office. In fact, once she and her father made amends enough, and he reinstated her trust fund, she could have had Benson, Benson, and Hart build her a nice high rise."

"She's humbled."

"She is. And she's right where she wants to be."

"I think that's a wonderful place to be. You're very lucky to have an idea of what you want to do."

"We'll see," he chuckled. "I've never been one to have a long term plan. I suppose I just always assumed BBH is where I'd end up."

"It speaks volumes that your father would let you do whatever you wanted."

His hand moved over hers in a gentle stroke. "What do you do?"

"Me? Oh, well that would depend on who you ask. My father would say I take care of my mother. My mother would say her job is to take care of me. I'd like to say I was a writer."

She felt him shift. "No kidding?" His voice rose in pitch. "I think that's very cool."

"You do?"

"Yes. What do you write?"

"Well," she cleared her throat. "I've written a lot of short stories. I write a blog, which no one but Fitz knew about."

"What kind a blog."

"The Blind Girl Diary. I write about the world of darkness from my perspective. I've done some series on how the blind are treated in restaurants, how people nearly fall over themselves when you go to a movie theater, and how I'd love to have a service dog as much for having help as companionship."

"Why don't you have one?"

"Remember, my mother thinks it's her job to guide me. I don't really need an actual service dog. There are a lot of people who need them. But a dog in general would be fun."

"How many followers do you have on this blog of yours?"

"Four thousand."

The car turned and she heard him laugh. "That's a lot of people."

"I suppose. I'd like to write articles. Maybe I'll be a published author someday. I've thought about writing books for young girls who are blind. You tend to go through a huge phase of assuming you're ugly since you can't see how your hair looks. You have to learn that it's how you feel that matters."

A moment later the car came to a stop. "We're here." She heard him turn in his seat and could feel the shift of his breath and knew he was facing her. She turned. "What about writing articles about charities? Interviews. Press releases? Do you think you could do that?"

A smile was tugging on the corners of her mouth. "You want me write about your aunt's organization?"

"Yeah. What if we got some media attention? Did some interviews with some of the women who she's helped? Get your name out there and find you four thousand more subscribers to your blog?"

A laugh burst from her. "You'd do that for me?"

"Of course." His hand came to her cheek and she reached for it. "Courtney, I don't know what this all is—these feelings I'm having. But I don't think there is much I wouldn't do for you."

He eased her toward him and his lips came to hers.

As he pulled away she sucked in a breath. "I'm never going to see again."

"Why did you say that?"

"If you continue to want to be with me, your life won't be everyday normal. My house has to be spotless or I'll get hurt. I can never drive to meet you anywhere. I sometimes put my shirt on backward," she thought of her mother's comments. "I have days where I get very depressed that I can't see the sunsets, the flowers bloom, or how my hair looks in the mirror. I'm a lot of work."

"You're a lot of wonderful, which I need in my life. If you're trying to make me change my mind it won't work. If you don't want to be with me because of all that, then fine. You make that decision. None of that fazes me. I'm done running from things I can't control, Courtney. It wasn't my style when I did it. Now, I'd like to take you into my house, which I hope is clean enough, and make you some dinner."

She let herself smile. "Thank you."

"No need. I want to see how far you're going to try to push

me. Something down in my gut tells me you can't make me run. I like you an awful lot."

His body moved and he opened his door. She sat a moment until he opened hers. It had only been a few days, but she knew what was brewing inside of her. She was scared to death of it, but it was there. Courtney would let it brew longer until she faced it. But she was fairly sure she was falling in love with this man she'd once thought smelled good—and he was so much more.

CHAPTER 23

*T*he house smelled freshly cleaned, and Courtney wondered if that had been what he'd done all day.

"This is the living room. The kitchen is just through here," he said as he led her behind the couch and to the kitchen. "The bathroom and laundry room are just down the hall. Bedrooms are upstairs and the basement is a separate apartment. I didn't realize the house was this small until I tried to explain it."

She smiled, feeling the grip of his hand pressed against hers. "And how many of you would live here at a time?"

"I guess at the most there were three of us. Clara and Christian lived upstairs, and I lived downstairs." He chuckled. "It's been a blessing that my aunt kept this house. It has come in handy."

"I think that's wonderful. It's a family tradition of sorts."

"Yeah. You're right." They walked further into the house and she heard him pull out a chair. "Here, have a seat. I'm going to start on dinner."

"I can help you."

"Oh, don't think you won't." He kissed her on the cheek. "But how about a glass of wine while I get it all pulled out?"

"I'd like that." She sat down in the chair. "So, you only have one brother?"

"Yes. Spencer. We're almost a year and a half apart."

"You've never known your life without him?"

"Right. He and our cousin Avery were born on the same day only minutes, or hours apart. I really don't remember. But they share the same birthday."

She laughed. "That's unique. I know you've told me you have a big family, but how many cousins do you have?"

He hummed and she knew he was thinking. "Only four. My father is an only child, so there are no cousins on that side."

"I don't have any cousins. My mother is an only child and so is my father. I don't know if I have cousins from my biological father."

She felt Tyler move next to her and set the glass on the table. "Your biological father?"

It was at that moment she realized she was more than a little comfortable around him. Never had she mentioned her biological father to anyone except when she was fighting with her mother.

"Yes. My mother was only sixteen when she had me. All I know about the man, whose hair color I share, is that he was military, too. I suppose her age and his might have been why he disappeared forever. That's about all I know."

"Does that bother you?"

"No. It's just something I can throw into an argument when I'm fighting with my mother."

"Do you fight a lot?"

She shrugged and felt for her glass. "I have a feeling we will for a bit." She took a sip. "Usually we have an okay relationship. We do get along. But the past year or two with me having more independence, well, I think that bothers her."

"So she'll get over it?"

She laughed. "I hope so. I plan to have a career, a husband, children—a life. She needs someone to take care of."

"Maybe she needs a career."

"She had one. When I lost my sight, she gave it up."

"And what did she do?"

Courtney sipped her wine again. "Financial planning."

"Fitzpatrick Financial?"

"Yes. She's the heir to the franchise. And beyond that—now I'm the heir."

She could hear Tyler move through the kitchen. He moved past her and set something in front of her. "Bowl in front of you. Head of lettuce to the side of you. Tear it up," he said with a laugh.

He moved back to the counter and she could hear him working on something else. Courtney situated the bowl and went to work on the head of lettuce.

"So, what about you? What kind of financial planner are you?" Tyler asked.

"My checkbook is in balance," she nearly snorted out a laugh. "I don't care anything about financial."

"You want to be a writer."

She tore a piece of lettuce and let it fall into the bowl. "Right."

Tyler began pounding something. It sounded as if he were fixing the kitchen.

"What are you doing?"

Tyler stopped. "Pounding chicken."

"What are you making?"

"Lemon garlic chicken. Sorry. I could have warned you."

"Never be sorry. I try not to let everything freak me out."

"I can see that." He went back to pounding the chicken. "So you'll be fine on Sunday, right?"

"Sunday?"

"Dinner, remember?"

Courtney nodded as she tore more leaves off of the head of lettuce. "You're going to introduce me to your perfect family."

"Right."

"You think they'll freak me out?"

He walked back and set down something on the table. "Oh, no. I think you're going to fall in love."

She continued to rip the lettuce and toss it into the bowl. With everything she had, she tried to keep her face calm and placid. She didn't want to think about falling in love with his whole family. That would certainly seal the deal—after all, every moment she spent with Tyler she knew she was falling in love him.

CHAPTER 24

*T*heir meal had been delightful. Tyler had surprised himself with garlic lemon chicken. He hoped he'd impressed her too, because he wasn't a chef.

They'd cleaned up after dinner and now sat on the front porch and listened to the kids play down the street.

"I think that is one of the happiest sounds," she said as she took a sip of her wine. "Fitz would always play in the street with his friends. You could hear him for miles."

"Spencer and I didn't get to do that. Of course the road up to our house is two miles long. So I suppose we had our own street to play on."

"I'll bet you had many things you did on that road that other kids couldn't do."

Tyler gave it some thought. "We had little go karts that we could drive and I suppose we wore out a few sets of tires on that road."

"See, Fitz couldn't have done that."

Tyler laughed. "It seems to me, he was the kind of kid who would have loved that."

She nodded. "He would have. My father was always so serious

with him, that Fitz really appreciated the moments when he could just be a kid."

"That would have been hard." In fact, Tyler couldn't even imagine. Even when telling his father that he didn't want to work for his company, his father understood. "What about you? What did the young Courtney do?"

She closed her eyes and took a deep breath. "I have boxes of pages that I wrote in braille." She opened her eyes and smiled. "That way my mother couldn't read it."

"Not all of us get to do things openly and yet secretly."

"I suppose. I won a poetry contest once. I wrote about Fitz."

"What did you write?"

Her smile widened. "I wrote about what a smelly boy he was."

Tyler burst out in laughter. "I'm sure he appreciated that."

"He did. I let him wear my medal around his neck." She let out a sigh. "He certainly kept things normal for me."

"And yet he blamed himself?"

She shrugged, the moment now growing dark. "It was always there. I don't blame him. How could I? But for as much joy as he always gave me, he wasn't so joyous."

"What do you mean?"

Courtney sipped her wine again. "My father is very strict. My mother, well, she's a bit needy in her own way. And Fitz had a lot of both of them. Add in a lifetime of guilt over my condition, and you end up with a very depressed young man. Oh, he didn't mope around or anything. In fact, if you met him you'd never know. But if you lived with him—well you get it."

"It's almost as if there is a glow to you when you speak of him."

"I loved him."

"You always will."

She turned her head toward him and held her hand out for him to take. "I really like you, Tyler Benson."

He swallowed hard. "I really like you too, Courtney Field."

"We're a unique twosome, aren't we? We both have trust funds that would keep us very comfortable and yet we aren't interested in the industry in which we could take over. We both would rather follow our hearts, and it's our heart that gets us in trouble."

"How could that get us in trouble?"

"You ran when yours got hurt."

"And you?"

"I tend to fall in love too fast."

"And that's bad?"

"Can be."

"You're afraid to fall in love with me?"

She licked her lips before she responded. "I'm vulnerable right now. Fitz is gone and he's been my pillar of strength for a very long time."

Tyler rubbed his thumb over her knuckles. "I think you've been your own."

"But, it isn't right for me to want to fall in love with you. Not when I've only known you a few days. Not when I spent the day of my brother's funeral kissing you."

"You want to fall in love with me?" He was inching in closer to her.

"Tyler, this is all very confusing. How could you want to fall in love with me? My family is all screwy. I'm in mourning, and any moment I'll burst into tears. And then there is the fact that I'll never see your face. How can you..."

Tyler moved in closer. "You really do talk too much." He lifted his hand to her cheek and pulled her to him. His lips brushed over hers with a need to make her understand that what was brewing in her was brewing in him too. There was no way he would say he loved her, not yet, but damn, he wasn't going to let her go. This was worth fighting for. He wanted this.

A moan escaped her throat and only made him want her

more. This wasn't what he'd expected when he'd moved back home.

He'd completely fallen in love with this woman who picked him up at the airport. It didn't matter to him that she'd never see his face. She seemed to see deeper inside of him than anyone ever had. All he had to do was prove to her that he wouldn't run. They were matched with their hearts, no matter the circumstances that brought them together.

First, he'd prove to her he could love her, and then he'd tell her. For now, he'd continue to kiss her breathless and hope that helped her understand.

CHAPTER 25

When Tyler walked through the front door of the Starbucks, in the Riverside Building that his father owned, he had a skip in his step and a whistle on his lips.

He'd stop by and say hello to his father later, but now he was going to meet with Avery and plan the gala of the year.

"You look too happy," his cousin said with her eyes narrowed on him.

"I am happy," he said and kissed her square in the middle of the forehead.

Tyler sat down in the chair across from her and studied her. Her dark hair matched her mother's—black, shiny, and long. However, her father's blue eyes peered out from dark lashes at him. If she weren't his cousin, she'd be someone he'd have taken a second glance at. Her cheeks had a rosy glow to them and that was because she was humored. Some things never changed.

Avery pushed a cup of coffee toward him. "I got your regular."

"You're the best."

Now she laughed. "Dear God, I don't remember the last time I saw you this happy. If this is what three years away does, I'm leaving tonight."

Tyler held his hands around the paper cup wrapped in a cardboard sleeve. "No, this is what coming home does. You're already here. No need to leave."

"I don't think this is all just coming home."

Tyler tried to hold in the smile, but how could he? "No, this is all about a woman."

Avery sat back in her chair, her legs crossed at the knee, and a perfectly manicured set of toes in a sandal bounced as she studied him.

"Darcy said you met a woman on the plane."

"I did."

"You went to her brother's funeral."

"Yep, that's her." Now the smile was free and he couldn't tuck it back.

"That's kinda sick."

Tyler leaned in. "No. And if you're thinking I took advantage of a situation, well I didn't. It just happened to be the reason she was on that flight and she asked me to be at the funeral."

"But you've been seeing her."

He sat back in his chair. "I have been. I'm bringing her to dinner on Sunday too."

"You really do like her."

"I do." Avery leaned in and took Tyler's hand. "I'm happy for you. Now tell me about her."

Tyler thought about it for a moment. What could he tell her? Would she simply take the word perfect and let that be the way it was, because in his mind that was the word that explained Courtney.

"I think you should just meet her."

"You're trouble, you know that?"

"I do. And now you have to work with me. So, tell me cuz, what do you have done so far? What needs to be done for this gala?"

129

Avery pursed her lips and sulked back in her seat. "I have the venue."

"Cool."

He waited for her to speak again. But she didn't.

The smile he'd felt pressed on his face began to diminish.

"That's all?"

"Don't judge me," she snapped. "I don't want to do this. This isn't my kind of work. I don't want to plan and promote."

"Then why did you tell her you would?"

"She's my mother." Avery took a sip of her iced coffee through a straw. "I don't know what I'm doing."

Tyler let out a deep and painful breath. "So we have three months to completely put the event together? Are you serious? Shouldn't something like this be planned for a year?"

Avery narrowed those blue eyes, which had gone icy, on him. "Next year you can start the day after. As for this year, we have three months. I told you, I don't want to do this."

Tyler bit the inside of his cheek. "Will you give me one hundred percent for three months? Please. I haven't been to one of these in years. I don't know what I'm getting into. Just be my partner for the next three months and we can do this."

She looked around and her mouth tightened and tensed. "What does your woman do? Maybe she can help too."

Tyler tapped his fingers on the table and the smile was back. "Maybe she could."

"I'll give you three months. But promise me I don't have to do this next year."

"If I don't get fired, you don't have to help me next year."

Now her eyes had lightened up and she sipped her coffee again. "Okay, good. So what are your thoughts on the event?"

CHAPTER 26

*C*ourtney closed her laptop and gave it a little pat. Tyler was going to either love what she'd done all day or be upset that she'd nosed her way into his aunt's business.

Since ten o'clock that morning, she had been on the phone with no less than a dozen women who now had secure jobs, good educations, and a healthy living environment because of *Simone Keller's Diamond Gift* organization.

Four of the women had gone on to marry men who were active in their community and owned their own businesses. Another three of them had businesses of their own. And Tyler had been right. The woman who had received the diamond earrings was in fact on the city council and running for a state position.

Courtney had always felt she'd accepted her fate fairly well. She'd adjusted, learned to deal with life in a new way at a young age, and she'd been told on more than one occasion that she'd helped someone else get through their trauma. But after having spent the day talking to the women whom Simone's organization had helped—she realized that being blind was a cakewalk.

Sure, she couldn't see the spring. Slippery sidewalks were her enemy. And it was very hard to run the path around the lake. But she'd done all of that. Never once in her life had she had a man beat her near to death and threaten her livelihood.

One woman had been stabbed four times and her child kidnapped by her ex-boyfriend. Now she lived in Washington D.C. and worked for better legislation against men like him.

It sent chills down Courtney's arms as she stood from her desk and stretched.

Taking her phone from her pocket, she checked the time. In the masculine British voice she'd programmed, her phone let her know that it was nearly six o'clock. That meant Tyler would be there soon. He'd promised her barbecue, and now she was starving for it.

COURTNEY WENT through her closet and pulled out her favorite pair of black jeans and a crisp white shirt. Fitz had never been a man of fashion, but he dated well. His last girlfriend had taken her shopping, and the ensamble was one of the outfits Missy had picked out.

She said it accentuated all the best parts classically. Courtney wasn't sure about that, but she felt good in the outfit and that meant a lot. And, with the buttons in the front she was fairly sure she wouldn't make the rare mistake of putting it on backward or inside out.

Once she was dressed, she dabbed on a little Chanel No. 5, which Fitz had also bought for her, and ran a brush through her hair. The only makeup she kept on hand was lip-gloss. She dabbed it onto her lips and made the pucker sound her mother had taught her to make.

The memory froze her in place. She'd been so hard on her mother for the past few weeks since they'd learned of Fitz's death. They'd argued and each had said nasty things to the other. Guilt was coursing through her veins now. Courtney had thrown her paternity in her mother's face and she hated when she did that. Everyone was due their mistakes. Even Courtney had had a few.

She heard the doorbell and she realized she needed to let go of the feelings she was having—for the moment anyway. There needed to be peace and acceptance between her and her mother. They were all they had now. There couldn't be any resentment.

Courtney walked down the steps, remembering to turn the lights on when she reached the bottom one.

"Tyler?" she called out before she answered the door.

"It's me."

She unlocked the locks and pulled open the door.

"Wow!" he said and she figured Missy must have been right. "You look amazing. I mean you always do, but wow."

"Thank you. I was hoping for that kind of reaction."

There was no movement for a moment and he said nothing.

"Is everything okay?" she asked, worried that something had slipped by her and he was upset.

"I'm just taking you in." Now he moved and he was quickly wrapping his arms around her and she around him. "I've thought of you all day. Is that crazy?"

"I hope not. I've done the same—thinking about you."

She felt his mouth move against her temple, to her cheek, to her neck, and then press against her lips.

Courtney swayed against him, pulling him close. His tongue teased. His breath warmed. His hands moved down her back and over the curve of her bottom.

She felt the moan escape as she heard it with her own ears. There was going to have to be a time, in this very fast paced relationship she was having, where she thought about what was to come next. She'd known Tyler Benson all of a week, but she knew she wanted his hands on her, his lips, his words.

Tyler's breath was heavy when he pulled back and rested his forehead against hers. "I guess I'm a little stirred up."

"We'd better go then—before we forget we had plans." She broke free from him and reached for her purse on the edge of the sofa. "I know this is bad etiquette, but do you mind if I take my laptop?"

"Are you going to do some work while we eat?"

"I did work, all day. And I want to show you."

"That's fine. Where is it? I can help you pack it up."

When he offered his help she didn't feel as though it was because she couldn't. It was exhilarating to think a man just wanted to help.

"It's on my desk in the corner. There is a small bag in the drawer next to it that I carry it in."

She could hear him move to the desk and pack up the computer.

"I'm anxious to see what you've done."

"You are?"

He stopped near her. "I'm trying real hard to make you under-stand that you're very important to me. Not just you, but every-thing you are and everything you do. Am I failing?"

She swallowed hard. "I'm just getting use to this kind of atten-tion, that's all."

"I have a lot more to give."

Her breath was shaky again. What was going to make this man break and leave? She'd always need something—even though she thought she'd proved to herself she didn't. Would he always be willing to be interested?

CHAPTER 27

*A*t the very moment the door opened, and Courtney stepped foot into Steve's Barbecue Pit and Beer, she could smell the familiarity. The stale scent of beer, cooked steak, fresh cornbread, and peanuts surrounded her. Dust lingered on the air from the thousands of garage sale decorations that adorned the walls. Hank rang out on the jukebox, and the heavy perfume of the woman walking toward them made her smile.

"Well, I'll be damned! Courtney Field, how are you, darlin'?"

"I'm well, Ms. Hilary."

"You are good with those voices aren't you?" The woman moved in closer and her fragrance grew heavier. "I'm really sorry to hear about your brother. He was a good boy."

"Thank you."

"Your mama and daddy must be very upset."

"My father is very proud of him, of course, even though you're correct, he's very sad. My mother, well, it'll take a long time I'm sure."

"Of course it will." Hilary placed her hand on Courtney's shoulder. "How are you dealin'?"

"One day at a time. Tyler here has been very supportive."

"You look awful familiar," Hilary said. "I've been here a hundred years, you belong to someone."

She heard Tyler chuckle and felt his arm move past her. Surely he was shaking Hilary's hand.

"Tyler Benson, I'm…"

"Oh, dear, Lord! You are Zach's son. Tyler's grandson."

"Yes, ma'am."

Courtney could hear the smile carry on his voice.

"You look just like your granddaddy. I served him a lot of ribs."

"I've always been told this was his favorite place."

"I'll be damned." Hilary made a little noise as if she were still looking at Tyler and taking in the sight of him. "Well, c'mon. I'll seat ya."

Tyler let Courtney take his elbow and he led her through the sounds of conversation, music, and children's laughter.

"It's a booth, is that okay?" he whispered in her ear.

"Fine." She felt the edge with her knee and slid on in, then felt him slide next to her, so she slid to the end.

"I'll be back in a few. What do you want to drink?" Hilary asked.

"I'll have a beer," Courtney said softly.

"I'll have one too," Tyler added.

"I'll be right back," Hillary confirmed as she hurried away.

Tyler leaned back against the booth and she could feel his eyes on her. She turned to face him.

"You're grinning, aren't you?"

"I'm still not sure you can't see sometimes. How do you know that?"

"There is a feel to it."

"Well then yes. I'm grinning," he admitted. "This whole town knows you, and you know each and every one of them by voice."

"Just as you'd know them by sight. Of course, Hilary's perfume gives her away first."

"I didn't smell her perfume."

Now Courtney laughed. She wondered how he'd missed it.

"So you look just like your grandfather, huh?"

"I've been told that on occasion."

"You never met him?"

"No. He died years before I was born. He had a heart attack while he and my grandmother were in New York."

She reached for his hand. "I'm sorry to hear that."

"I know she's tried to move on, but I think my grandmother misses him still."

"If someone is your true love, I don't suppose you ever move on."

He gave a hum and she could hear the menu brush against the table.

"What do you get here?" she asked trying to clear the air again.

"I was thinking that barbecue platter for two."

"Alright, but I warn you, I'm a messy rib eater."

He set the menu down on the table and lifted his hand to her cheek. "Are you tempting me?"

"With what?" Her voice had gone airy having him touch her in public.

"Wanting to lick it off your lips."

She caught the breath that tried to escape just as Tyler pulled back his hand and Hilary set their beers on the table.

Tyler ordered and Hilary walked away.

"So what were you going to show me?" he asked as he took a drink of his beer. She could smell it as it transferred from his glass to his lips.

"Um—I..." She tried to gather her thoughts, but all she could think about was his tongue on her skin. His hands. His words.

She squeezed her eyes and clenched her stomach. They'd have to discuss it. Where was this going and was it going right where she wanted it to go?

Courtney collected herself and pulled her computer from the bag on the seat next to her.

She felt for her beer, pushed it back, and opened the laptop. "Here. Read this. What do you think?"

Tyler moved the laptop and Courtney reached for her beer. She sipped, and waited, and sipped again.

"Well?"

"Hold on. I'm not a very fast reader," he said.

Courtney sipped at her beer again, then set it down and rested her anxious hands in her lap. Finally, she heard him lower the lid of the computer.

"It sucks?"

"What?" He turned to her. "No. God, no! It was...I didn't know...I'm..." he let out a breath and then sucked one in. "I'm in over my head. I didn't know some of these women went through all that."

"What did you think?"

"I didn't know. I knew some were homeless. Some were abused, but..." He reached for her hand and brought it to the top of the table. "You took time to find these women and talk to them?"

"Yes."

"Where did you find them?"

"I searched. These are specifically women who had something about the *Diamond Gift* in their profiles on social media or business sites."

"That one woman was stabbed."

"She was the most dynamic one to talk to. She was an alcoholic and a heroin user. She now works in D.C. trying to change the laws."

"We need to invite all these women to the gala."

"They all said I could contact them. I have permission from all of them to publish their stories."

He'd grown quiet again, but she was quickly learning this meant he was deep in thought.

"Will you work with me?" Tyler asked.

CHAPTER 28

*C*ourtney replayed his question in her head. "Me? You want me to work with you? How?"

"Avery hates planning these things. She's promised to show me the ropes, but I want to do this long term. I want to help my aunt raise as much money, and bring as much attention to this organization as I can. She's done a great job up till now, but now there are stories to back it all up. Look at these successes. Over twenty years of successes. You brought this to light for me, and very well I might add."

"Thank you."

"You're very gifted, Courtney. If I was a man to cry in public, I would have."

She felt her cheeks grow warm. "You should read my fiction."

He chuckled. "What kind of fiction?"

"I have a variety of romantic suspense, contemporary romance, and I have some paranormal."

"Just paranormal? No romance."

"Think about it. Every book you've ever read probably had an element of romance or relationship."

He thought hard about it. "I have to go back quite a long way to think about a book where there wasn't some kind of chemistry."

She smiled. "Anyway," she leaned in closer to his ear, "Let's say my imagination is very vivid and if you think you'd cry over this, I can guarantee you a full out blush."

Tyler laughed, kissed her on the cheek, and picked up his beer. "I think this relationship is going to be fun."

Her heart stalled and then kicked back up. "Relationship?"

"Isn't that what we have? Forgive me if I'm wrong." His voice hitched and he set down his beer. "I haven't done a ton of dating, but we are dating right?"

"It seems like it."

"And I want to be with you. Do you want to be with me?"

"Of course." How could he possibly think any differently? She was more worried he'd want to ease her back into society and move on after her grief had subsided.

"Then can we say we're dating? Tomorrow, when I introduce you to my parents, can I say you're my girlfriend?"

Now she giggled. "Sounds elementary doesn't it?"

"I don't know any other way. I told you. I'm not good at this."

Courtney let her hand run up his arm until she reached his neck and she cupped her fingers there. "I think you're very good at this." She licked her lips and moved even closer. "Tyler, will you stay with me tonight?"

His breath had grown hot against her cheek. "Are you sure?"

"I don't think I've ever been more sure about anything."

"I want to."

She brushed his lips with hers. "Then I guess you can tell your parents I'm your girlfriend. It looks like we're going to make that very official."

"Suddenly I'm thinking we should take all this food home."

Courtney eased back. It was settled. She was fully in love with this man.

. . .

HILARY HAD ARRIVED with their food about the time they'd considered having her just pack it up. But when Tyler heard Courtney's stomach rumble, and she'd admitted she hadn't eaten all day, he decided that the evening ahead would come soon enough. After all, they'd just settled it—very elementary as she'd put it—she was his girlfriend and that meant to him she wasn't going anywhere.

Had all of this been some kind of bigger power at play? He wondered as he took a rib and pulled the first bite off with his teeth. Had he needed to leave the comforts of home and travel the world so that he'd come back at the very right time? Would he have made these career choices if he'd have stayed? Would he have found a woman already in Nashville, or was he destined to find this one?

What wasn't to love about her, he thought as he watched her devour her first rib. Courtney had accepted a horrible fate and yet it didn't seem as though she saw it that way at all. And through her, he'd learned to accept. It had been nearly immediately that he'd chosen to go right to his sister and ask for her forgiveness. He owed that to Courtney. Her way of seeing the world made him see it too. He was the damned luckiest man on the planet.

She turned to him. "I should have thought better about this when I put on this white shirt. One of those things about being blind. I never know if my clothes are ruined."

Tyler lifted his napkin to the corner of her mouth. "I'll tell you what. You write me stories, and I'll tell you if your laundry is stained."

"Stories?"

"If you can write newsworthy pieces like you did about *Diamond Gift*, I have no doubt you could be a bestselling author. And I'm sure between my grandmother, father, and numerous aunts, someone knows someone in the book industry. Even Clara might. Song writing isn't too far off—I wouldn't think."

"You'd make my dreams come true and tell me when my laundry is stained?"

"I'd do that."

"I love you, Tyler." She shook her head and he wanted to respond, but she turned her head down. "Sorry. That was supposed to stay in my head." She turned back toward him. "Do me a favor and don't say it back. No matter what. Right now, don't say it."

"Even if I'm thinking it?"

"Especially."

"Okay then, I won't say it. And yes, I'd love to see your dreams come true. Something tells me it would only make the glow in your cheeks more brilliant."

CHAPTER 29

Courtney held her computer in her lap as Tyler drove toward her house. The air between them was thick. Dinner had been wonderful. Conversation was easy. But she'd invited him to stay, and they were headed home.

Stay certainly didn't mean, come in for coffee. Stay to her had meant *share my bed. Hold me in my bed. Make love in my bed.*

Not one ounce of regret pulsed through her, but she couldn't speak for him.

"I'm going to stop at the store here on the corner and run in real quick. Can I get you anything?" he asked and she felt the car pull out of traffic.

"No. I'm fine."

"I'll hurry." He parked the car and quickly jumped out.

She should have asked him for something to help take care of her nerves, which threatened to make her sick. Was there a way to make this night perfect? That was what she wanted. But they were going in together. She couldn't have set it all up. Made sure the sheets were clean. Hell, she didn't even know if the pillowcases matched.

Then again, did it matter?

Had she done all of that, there would be no spontaneity either. This was better. She had to remind herself that she'd only known Tyler a week. Okay, so she'd fallen head over heels in love with him in a week, and now she was taking him to bed. But, preparedness was good. He was still a stranger and she needed to keep that in mind. She needed her senses to be sharp. Fitz had taught her that.

Tyler was true to his word and back in the car only a few minutes later.

"What is that smell? Is that a bouquet of flowers?" Her voice lifted as she heard the rustling of cellophane.

"Can't very well take a girl home and not give her flowers. And here." He handed her the flowers and another box. "I got you candy too. Seriously, I'm trying to pack in as much as I can in one week."

She couldn't help it. She burst into laughter. "Are you always this wonderful at putting people at ease?"

"No. Don't go thinking this is my calling."

She felt the car move backward. "Oh, I don't know. You were very calm on the plane. You helped me through the funeral. Came to my rescue when I needed you to go through my brother's things. And now you bought me flowers and candy to ease me through my invitation of taking you home."

"Good, you think I'm some hero. I'm just a nervous guy trying not to act that way."

The laughter came harder now and her heart was squeezing a little tighter when she thought about him. Perhaps this night was going to be perfect after all.

TYLER PULLED up in front of Courtney's house and turned off the engine.

"I know you've invited me, and believe me I want to take you up on this invitation. But, I'd never hold it against you if you changed your mind."

Courtney took a moment to assess her thoughts. The cellophane wrap around the flowers and the candy brushed against the bag her laptop was stowed in. She could back out if she wanted to. He was giving her a moment and she knew in her heart that he'd come back if she said to.

Courtney turned her face toward him. "Tyler, come inside. I want to be with you. And I don't just mean emotionally anymore. I want to be with you physically."

Her voice shook, but she heard his door open and close. A moment later, her door opened.

Tyler's hands came right to her face and his mouth quickly moved against hers. Tyler's tongue sought hers out and a moan escaped him—and then her.

Tyler took the roses from her hand and then the box of candy. She knew he'd placed them on the dashboard.

"We'll come back for those." He unbuckled her seatbelt and his arm came up under her legs and the other around her shoulders.

"What are you doing?"

"Carrying you up those steps. I'm a hero and all, remember."

"My laptop," she said, gripping it.

"Hold on to it tight." Tyler's mouth was on hers again and her mind swirled vividly in color.

He lifted her out of the car and shoved the door closed with his hip.

Courtney wrapped one arm around his neck and held tight to her laptop with the other, all the while making work of her lips against the pulse in his neck.

"Door," he muttered. "Door. Where are your keys?"

That brought on a laugh. "My purse. I think it's in the car."

"Damn. So much for sexy entrance, huh?" He set her down on wobbly legs. "I'll be right back."

She heard him run down the steps, pull open the door to the car, and run back up.

"Here's your purse." He set it in her hands and she quickly went about searching for them in their assigned space.

Courtney felt for the lock, slid in the key, and turned. When the door pushed open, her legs were scooped out from under her again and she was carried into the house.

Tyler closed the door with his body as they entered the house with his mouth moving against hers.

"My laptop," she mumbled against his lips and he set her down.

She handed it to him and felt him take it, but he never moved from her, which meant he'd only set it on the steps or on the couch. What did it matter? His hands were back on her, arms wrapped around her, lips pressed against hers.

She swallowed the taste of him, the warmth, and the feel. This wasn't something she'd done lots of times before, but she'd been with a few men and all of them had been in the same boat she was in—they felt their way through it.

Tyler had a unique advantage at this point—or perhaps she did. He could see everything and she couldn't. The thought was there. She'd never know if he had a certain scar or mole that made him less attractive. In her mind he was a god.

He, however, would see all her imperfections—even the ones she knew nothing about. This would be a truthful moment— she sucked in a breath of courage. There would be no loss, she told herself, if he walked away. Nothing ventured, nothing gained.

Tyler pulled back. "Are you okay? You're tensing up."

"I can't see you."

He let out a chuckle. "I know that."

"I mean, what if I take my clothes off and you don't like what you see?"

Tyler's hands came to her shoulders and rested there for a

moment before moving down her arms. He captured her hands in his.

"I hope you don't think I'm petty like that."

She shook her head. "If you were you wouldn't be here." She knew that to be truth enough.

"Courtney, you're the most beautiful woman I've ever known, inside and out. I don't have to keep touching you or take you to bed to know how I feel about you." She heard him let out what could be construed as a moan. "Of course, I'm also a man, and I want to."

She stepped in closer to him. "I've never been with a man who could see."

"I could tie something over my eyes."

That had her laughing now and she eased against him. "Maybe someday and only if I'm driving your car."

Tyler pulled back now. "You want to drive?"

"I never have."

"Hmm. Interesting thought." He moved back against her. "We can plan that later. Are we together on me carrying you up those stairs?"

Courtney took in a deep breath and let it out slowly. "I've never wanted anything more," she said.

Quickly, his mouth was back on hers and he scooped her up again.

"Good. After all, I am a man and I'm dying here."

CHAPTER 30

*T*yler lay next to Courtney, his arm tucked up under her, her hair sprawled out over his chest and the pillow.

His chest heaved from the breath he tried to capture in his lungs.

Sweat glimmered on Courtney's skin. Her heart raced against his chest, and her breath warmed his skin. Not only had he seen every inch of her more-than-perfect body, he'd touched it, and tasted it. She'd quivered under his touch, moaned under his tongue, and stifled the scream he'd brought out in her by biting down on his shoulder as he'd spilled over from what she'd done to him.

Tyler had been glad he'd had the foresight to stop at the corner store and buy a box of condoms. It had been awhile since he'd been with a woman. There wasn't a supply of them tucked in his wallet or car.

He thought about the moment he'd stopped what they'd been doing and reached for the box he'd shoved in his jean pocket. For a moment, he'd thought Courtney was going to cry because he'd even given thought of protecting her—them.

She moaned against his skin. "I've never felt like that before."

Tyler brushed her hair from her forehead. "You're going to explode my ego."

"It deserves it." She pressed a kiss to his chest. "I never thought someone would take such care of me. I mean you carried me up the stairs. You didn't just have sex with me."

Tyler ran a hand down her back. "You're more than that to me."

"I just keep waiting for the moment when that's all I am."

"It's not going to happen." Tyler pressed a kiss to her forehead.

"I believe that from you." She lifted her head. "I've always accepted what happened to me. It sucks. Don't get me wrong. It might have been better if I hadn't always known what being sighted was like. But it happened. I am who I am because of it."

She trailed her fingers down his breastbone and back up. "And I believe the world is full of good people. You know, the kind that don't judge a person's ability on whether they can see or not. But I've learned that people in general are not patient enough for people like me."

Tyler rolled her so that she was on her back and he was looking down at her. "I'm a very patient person." He laid his lips on the crevice of her neck and trailed more over her shoulder. "You'll meet my family tomorrow, and you'll understand where I get my patience."

Courtney smiled as he moved his mouth back to hers. "Your family won't judge me?"

"No. Not a one of them. Talk about a group that accepts anyone—everyone. My mother, aunt, and uncle were adopted. My sister was given up for adoption and then reunited with our family—so I consider her adopted back," he said and she giggled under him. "My Aunt Simone was as far from normal as I suppose you could get for my uncle. And Warner Wright..." He propped himself up on his arm and thought. "I think he was lucky he landed in this family where everyone is accepted. He needed that."

"And what about Tyler Benson? The son who felt pushed out when his sister came back? Is he accepted in this family?"

He ran his fingers through her hair and focused on the softness of each strand against his skin.

"Tyler Benson was the only one who thought he didn't fit in. He'd never been unaccepted," he said as if he were realizing it for the first time too.

"That's what I figured."

"You're going to love them. All of them."

"Do you suppose they're going to know what's going on here —between us?"

He chuckled as he nuzzled his face into her hair, which sprawled out like a fan. "Something tells me you'll still have that glow in your cheeks by dinner time tomorrow."

Courtney's mouth opened. "Glow? Why?"

Tyler pressed his mouth to hers and took it with the passion that surged through him. "Because I'm thinking that this is exactly where I want to be all day, doing exactly this," he said kissing her again. "Chances are they might notice."

He felt Courtney tense again beneath him, but as his tongue tangled now with hers and her body began to go pliant under his, he was sure she too wouldn't care what kind of glow she gave off. The Keller/Benson clan was about to fall in love with the most perfect woman Tyler had ever known.

CHAPTER 31

*E*very muscle in Courtney's body was relaxed, until the car stopped and she heard Tyler put it in park.

"This is it."

She heard him pull the keys from the ignition. "I've only known you a week. Maybe it's too early to meet your family."

"I've already met yours."

That was true enough. Thankfully she'd managed to avoid them most of the week. Well, her father at least. She knew that wasn't going to last long. He'd already texted her and asked for her to meet with him on Monday.

She wasn't going to tell Tyler about that. After she heard what her father had to say, then she'd see how she felt about sharing the conversation.

"I don't take you as the type of person who gets nervous," Tyler said resting his hand on her thigh.

"Oh, I can get nervous. In fact, I'm very nervous."

Tyler moved in his seat and she could feel his eyes on her so she turned her head toward him. "What are you nervous about? Give me specifics and I'll be able to tell you what to expect."

Courtney dropped her shoulders. "Did you tell your family I'm blind?"

"No."

"Why?"

"Because that doesn't define you. Would you have rather I had?"

She shrugged. "Even when people know in advance, it doesn't stop the shock."

"My grandmother has met you. My guess is she might have mentioned it to my parents. Not because it matters, but because you see the world differently than the rest of us. It's a charming quality."

That squeezed at her heart. "I've been told I don't look blind."

Tyler's hand came to her cheek. "You don't. I can tell you that. Your eyes are clear, chocolate brown with specks of gold in them. You often look deep in thought."

Courtney bit down on her lip. That was probably the sweetest thing anyone had ever said to her. "Someone in that house will stop mid-sentence when they notice me."

"Okay, so someone will. I can absolutely guarantee that it will be only a heartbeat long and never happen again."

"You can guarantee that?"

"With this group, yes."

Courtney licked her lips. "I'm scared of your mother."

Tyler laughed at that and she didn't know if she should be horrified because he thought it was funny or maybe it was something she should be afraid of.

"My mother? Oh, my. No one in their life could possibly be afraid of my mother."

"You've never been afraid of her? You ran away after all."

His laughter stopped. She'd wounded him. But she couldn't help it.

"I left because she'd hurt me. Not because she was mean. I was wrong to run away—hide—leave. Whatever the hell I did."

"I'm sorry," she said softly. She was on edge. This was what she'd do to her mother, not her lover. "Let's just say I'm afraid she won't think I'm worthy."

"I think you are, and that will sell it. What else?"

"Will your cousin Christian be there?"

"Y—es," his word was drawn out.

"And his sister Clara and her husband?"

"More than likely. At least she will be. He's still working a lot. Why do you ask?"

"Fitz admired Christian. I want to tell him that."

Tyler took her hand and gave it a squeeze. "Chris has gone through a lot the past few years. That will mean a lot to him."

Courtney smiled. "And Clara and Warner are famous."

He chuckled at that. "They are my family. In this house they clean the dishes, pass the bread, and give me a hard time. In this house they aren't famous."

"I'll try not to be star struck."

"It'll be easy enough."

She took a deep breath to calm her nerves. "What about you? What do you expect? I've known you all of a week."

"I expect them to love you."

"I mean, if I go in here, do you expect more from me?"

His body moved and she knew she'd made him uncomfortable. "I don't understand."

"This relationship is new. I've said things out loud to you that I should have saved in my own head. I've gone to bed with you."

"We're adults. That's allowed."

"I don't know what I can give you, emotionally. I don't want to set you up and fail you."

"I'll be the judge of whether I feel failed. God, who put it in your head that you weren't worthy of love and attention? Certainly not Fitz."

No, certainly not him, she thought. "I deserve to be reserved."

"Fine. Be reserved on the basis that you're meeting new

people. Be a bit nervous that the man who loves you is about to introduce you to his mother. But don't go in thinking they will judge you because you can't see their faces. That sells you short."

"Go back." Her breath was stuck in her chest. "The man that what?"

Tyler took both her hands in his. "The man that loves you. I know you don't want to hear it, but it's there. I wouldn't have taken you to bed any other way. I'm not like that. I wasn't raised like that."

"And I don't usually use my blindness as a crutch."

"I didn't think you did."

"I'm really nervous."

Tyler leaned in and pressed a kiss to her lips. "Do you love me?"

"Yes," she said and there was no hesitation in it.

"Then you will love them and they will love you. You don't have to see them to know. This family loves with all their heart and unconditionally."

Was it too much, she wondered, to want that as badly as she wanted Tyler in her life?

TYLER WALKED around the car and opened her door. She stepped out and let her cane open. She didn't use it in her home and hadn't used it when she was with him at dinner. He could see this was a moment when she needed that security. Her cane provided that to her. Perhaps it would ease things a bit too. If he knew his family, someone already had their nose pressed to the window waiting for them. They'd see the cane. They'd know she was blind. They'd be prepared if his grandmother hadn't mentioned it.

How much of that had she planned when she'd pulled the cane out of her purse, he wondered.

It wasn't any more of a surprise when the front door opened

and Clara grinned down at him. "Two weeks in a row!" She shouted. "And thank God you brought a woman."

Courtney pinched his elbow and he fought back the urge to yelp, but he saw the smile on her face and that told him already she was prepared to meet his family.

"How come you're the only one who stands at the door?" he asked as they made it up the walk.

"Warner is on his way. He finished his solo album." Her voice carried with it the pride that her eyes carried.

"Solo?" Courtney stopped. "Why is he going solo? You're a fantastic duo."

Tyler moved so that Courtney's grip was no longer on his arm and he laced his arm behind her. "Clara, this is my girlfriend Courtney. She's a big fan of yours."

Courtney slapped him on the chest. "Big fan, yes. Girlfriend, we'll see," she said laughing as Clara walked down the steps toward them.

"She fits right in," Clara said easily. "I'm the oaf's cousin."

Courtney reached out her hand and Clara shook it.

"We thought he was bringing someone with him. I'll admit I was the look out," Clara said.

"I thought you were waiting for me." The voice came from the street and Clara's eyes lit up.

"Come here!" Clara shouted as Warner walked up to them. "This is Tyler's girlfriend, Courtney."

He watched as Warner processed Courtney's hand extended, but her eyes diverted toward his shoulder. He shook her hand graciously.

"Very nice to meet you."

Courtney smiled wide. "I'm a bit star struck," she admitted. "I don't mean to be. I told Tyler I was afraid I would be."

Tyler gave her a gentle squeeze.

"I'm star struck too," Warner said. "My wife is amazing. She has the voice of an angel and the body of a goddess."

Courtney laughed and Warner took her hand and draped it over his arm. "C'mon, let's go inside."

Courtney shifted from Tyler to Warner. "Let me take your elbow and how many steps are there?" she asked as she collapsed the cane and let it fold up in her hand.

"There are three," Warner answered.

"Wonderful." She turned her head toward Tyler. "Come along, Tyler. Warner Wright is going to escort me in." Her voice was full of humor and lightness. She was star struck, and he thought perhaps Warner was too. Not only over his wife, but Courtney seemed to have wormed her way right into the man's heart just as she had Tyler's.

A flash of—something—hit him in the chest. He was going to marry that woman, he thought. Oh, yeah. She was absolutely the one.

CHAPTER 32

*V*oices, laughter, and the hum of the television filled Courtney's ears. Something fragrant—Italian—filled her nose. Sausage, tomato, there was chicken, and the ever wonderful scent of fresh bread.

Warner warned her of the step up into the house. She was in an entrance hallway. This she could tell without her cane. The area was tighter.

The voices became muffled and then there was the sound shuffling of feet.

"Okay, Warner has a new girl," a man said with a laugh as he moved toward them.

"I stole her from Tyler," Warner replied. "This is Courtney."

"Hello," she said and held her hand out to shake the man's hand.

His grip was firm, but friendly. "Nice to meet you. I'm Christian."

Courtney felt her heartbeat kick up a notch. "Christian Keller?"

He chuckled. "Yes."

"Sorry." She caught her breath. "My brother was a big fan of yours. He enjoyed watching you play ball."

"Oh." His voice shook a bit. "I haven't played ball in a long time."

"I know. But I wanted you to know you brought him great joy."

Christian patted her hand. "I'm sorry about your brother. His sacrifice to our country won't be forgotten."

Courtney stiffened her trembling lips. "Thank you. I appreciate that."

"Okay, okay." Tyler moved in next to her and placed his hands on her shoulders. "Let's move into the house. I can smell dinner and my stomach is growling. Where is my mother?"

"She's right here," a woman said and Tyler gave Courtney's shoulders a squeeze.

"There she is." Tyler moved around her and toward the woman, leaving one hand on Courtney's arm as he embraced the woman.

"Mom, this is Courtney," Tyler said as he wrapped his arm tightly around her.

"Hello, Mrs. Benson. It's nice to meet you," Courtney offered as she held her hand out to shake his mother's.

"Oh, aren't you precious." His mother took her hand, and instead of shaking her hand, his mother held it in hers, patting it with her other hand. "I'm so excited to finally meet you."

A moment later she was pulled into an embrace by the woman who smelled of floral notes and kitchen scents.

"Welcome." She pulled back. "And you can call me Regan. I'd prefer it." She stepped in next to Courtney and whispered in her ear, "Mrs. Benson is my mother-in-law."

Courtney laughed. "She is a very sweet woman."

"Hmmm, yes. She said she met you first, and you were quite a catch."

Courtney laughed. Okay, there had been no reason for her to be nervous about meeting his mother.

"Come, I want my parents to meet you."

Regan moved in next to her and offered her arm just as Tyler had the first time he'd walked with her. Courtney took her elbow and let her lead her through the house.

Within minutes, Courtney had met every single member of Tyler's family. Her head spun with names and voices. Laughter ensued, again peace filled her heart.

TYLER WATCHED Courtney as she engaged in conversation with the women he called family. They'd sat her down at the kitchen table. She was nestled in between Avery and Simone. His mother and grandmother were busy at the stove with his aunt Madeline.

He'd missed this. This was where he belonged and looking at Courtney laughing with his cousin, he knew it was where she belonged too.

"Hey, cuz," Ed slapped Tyler on the shoulder. "I need some help bringing in the cooler of beer. Help me out."

Tyler nodded and walked to Courtney. "I'm going to step out back with Ed."

"I'm in good hands. Don't worry about me," she said in his ear and gave him a kiss on the cheek.

Tyler walked out the back door with his cousin and out toward the detached garage.

"Why don't you guys do dinner somewhere bigger? I mean you have to keep the beer in a cooler and bring it in?" Tyler asked as he followed Ed.

"While Grandma and Grandpa can still come, dinner is here. Besides, I think Darcy really enjoys this. I know she had a good upbringing, but she didn't have family like this. She craves it." Ed opened the cooler and pulled out two beers. He handed one to

Tyler and twisted the cap off his own. "We put in an application for adoption last week."

"Adoption? So you're ready to start a family?"

"We're ready."

"What about your own? Can't you have kids of your own?"

Ed pulled from his beer. "Oh, we plan to do that too. Darcy feels like it would be the right thing to do. With your mom and my dad having been adopted, and Aunt Arianna. And with her having been adopted, she just feels like we should give a home to someone who needs it."

The thought spun inside Tyler. And these were the people he came from, he considered. The kind of people who would do for others first. Pride swelled in him.

"I think that's a real nice idea." He twisted off the cap of his own beer. "Are you going to try to have your own kids soon?"

Ed wiggled his eyebrows. "We try every chance we get." He laughed and Tyler followed suit. "What about you and this new woman? You've been home a week."

"Sounds like fate brought me back, huh?"

"This is the woman you met on the plane? The one whose brother died?"

"Yeah, that's her."

Ed considered. "Darcy told me about her. That's sad about her brother."

"She's dealing with it well enough, I think. I mean, I can't imagine if something happened to Spencer or to Darcy—or to any of you."

"Maybe she should talk to Tori. She lost her sister and her brother-in-law. Maybe they would connect."

"Maybe," he said giving it some thought. "They do have a lot in common."

"Was she born blind?" Ed asked and Tyler wondered how long he'd been holding on to that. It was a natural question, he supposed.

"No. When she was eight she was kicked by a horse. It caused her to lose her sight."

"That's horrible."

Tyler shrugged. "Not to hear her talk about it. I mean, she wouldn't have wished it on herself, but she's no less a person because of it."

"She's beautiful and she fits in well. I'd say you did good."

"She did good. She made a move on me." He laughed. "I smelled good."

Ed chuckled too. "You're in love with her."

Tyler looked up from his beer. "Completely." He took a sip and then let out a long breath. "I'm not dumb though. I know she has a lot of healing to do over her brother. But after I met her, I had a renewed sense of what I was supposed to do. I drove right here to see Darcy last week. And when I came to see you all about a job—suddenly I knew that wasn't what I wanted."

Ed rested his hand on Tyler's shoulder. "She's good for you. And I think you'll be good for her too. C'mon, let's get this in the house."

They each picked up a handle of the cooler and carried it back to the house where Tyler could hear laughter flow—specifically Courtney's.

He and Ed set the cooler by the back door. One thing about her not seeing him in the kitchen was it didn't distract her from her conversation. Avery had exchanged seats with Christian's wife Tori. They were holding hands, heads nearly pressed together, and they were talking. There were tears. There were smiles. There were laughs.

Ed had been right. They would connect and it seemed to be good for both of them. How amazing was this family? He should have remembered how amazing they were. They had already taken Courtney under wing and embraced her. Wouldn't they have done that for him too? He'd isolated himself over his mother's confessions. He'd let himself cut off his entire existence from what he'd known.

Guilt threatened to choke him. Not once had he taken the time to think about what she'd gone through before he selfishly took himself out of the picture and decided he needed time to process what his mother had done—to him.

A bead of sweat formed on his brow and he quickly wiped it away. What could she possibly have had to endure to give away a child?

CHAPTER 33

*a*s Courtney's laughter rang out, it pulled Tyler from his spiral of pity. It was his mother now seated next to her, where Simone had been. She was leaned in close to her, and each of them wore a smile that turned their cheeks high and their eyes bright.

Courtney was right. She didn't look blind. Her eyes danced on the story his mother told her and her laughter only brightened them. He reminded himself that only a week ago she'd been on an airplane that carried the body of her brother and yet here she was laughing and enjoying the life she had.

It was quite obvious that Courtney no longer feared his mother.

Spencer moved in next to Tyler, opened the cooler, and retrieved a beer. He twisted off the top and nudged his brother.

"Is it a sign when your mother takes to your girlfriend like that?"

Tyler shrugged. "I never really brought anyone home to her before. Not anyone of significance."

Spencer laughed. "Tonya Kincade."

That caused Tyler to snort a laugh. "You thought that was significant?"

"I did. What were you, seventeen? So I was sixteen?"

"Yeah, so?"

"So," Spencer drew out the word as he drummed his fingers against the bottle of his beer. "She was about a foot taller than you and was very well endowed."

"You're a pig," Tyler joked as he pulled from his beer. "But you're right. If I remember correctly that was all she had going for her."

"Maybe at the time."

Tyler turned and looked at his brother who swept his dark hair back with a shake of his head.

"She's not as dim as I think she was?"

Spencer laughed. "Dr. Kincade. Okay, she's not a doctor yet, but she's in med school. Uncle Curtis told me he'd run into her. Pediatrics."

"Good for her." Tyler meant it. He didn't really remember much about her, but he did remember her taking a very long time to understand that he wanted more than star gazing in the back of his car.

He thought about that for a moment. Maybe she wasn't so dim. Somehow, he remembered, that very endowed young woman took their conversation and hungry kisses down another path, so to speak. By the end of the night he hadn't done more than kiss her, her virginity and his were both intact, and he'd gone home not even upset that she'd led him on and he'd gone home without any kind of manly reward.

It had been a long time since he'd thought about her or any other woman for that matter. And wasn't it interesting that as he stood there listening to his lover's laugh mix with his mother's, he realized this was a memory he'd keep.

"So you're working with Simone now, huh?" Spencer asked.

Tyler nodded, breaking thoughts that had kept him silent for a moment. "Feels like the right thing to me."

"Good. You'd be in my way anyway." Spencer smiled behind his bottle as he sipped his beer.

Tyler laughed. Could they be more different? His hair was light, Spencer's was dark like their mother's. Tyler's eyes were blue. Spencer's were brown. A year in age separated them, and about four inches in height, in Tyler's favor.

Spencer had a mind for business, and Tyler's mind tended to wander.

At the moment it wandered back to Courtney who was now engaged in a conversation with his grandmother who had taken a seat at the small table across from her.

"Where all have you lived?" His grandmother's voice shook with her many years.

"Oh," Courtney pushed back her shoulders and considered. "Germany, Japan, a short time in England, and a few weeks in Italy."

"A few weeks?"

"Yes. About the time we got settled they decided to send us back to America."

"It's been a lifetime since I've been to Europe." His grandmother sighed. "I'm happy to have those memories."

"As am I," Courtney said.

"Have you always been without your sight?" His grandmother asked and it seemed as though the room stilled.

Tyler took one step toward the table when he noticed Courtney's smile. "No. I was eight. I can remember colors and un-aged faces. My last visual memory is of my brother. He was four and we'd picked my mother a bouquet of wild daises."

"That's beautiful," his mother said softly.

"So your sight," his grandmother reminded her of the conversation that seemed to have skewed.

Tyler took one more step toward the table, but his grandmother looked up at him as though he was intruding and he stepped back.

"Well, my sight was lost after an accident with a horse. See, my father was very fond of horses and raised us around them. I have a grand appreciation of them," she said and Tyler thought of her nuzzling her cheek against the horses in his grandmother's barn.

"Anyway, my brother happened to frighten one we were grooming. I was unlucky enough to be in the wrong place. The horse kicked me in the head. I was knocked to the ground and was unconscious."

"That's terrible," Avery covered her mouth as she stood at the edge of the table near the women.

"It caused severe nerve damage and I've never seen again." Courtney smiled as she spoke. "Oh, I can see dark and light. I know day and night. And in my mind everything is more vivid in color than I know it is in actuality. I get to make it all beautiful."

There were smiles on the women who surrounded her. He could imagine that not one of them would ever look at something and think it plain again.

CHAPTER 34

*T*he small house, which had once been Tyler's grandparent's house and now was home to Ed and Darcy, was full of family. There were two card tables added to the extended dining room table. Folding chairs had been added alongside of the formal dining room chairs.

Laughter and noise carried through the house like a song, Tyler thought. How could he have forgotten that this was paradise?

Breadbaskets were passed and pasta was lopped onto plates.

Tyler filled Courtney's plate with everything she'd given a nod to and then explained where it was situated on the plate.

She leaned in close to him until her lips pressed to his ear. "I'm in love with each and every one of these people."

He took her hand, smiling. "I think the feeling is mutual."

As conversations started back up, Ed and Christian stood, pulling Clara up with them. Ed tapped his glass, Christian tried to clear his throat, and Clara stood staring at her brothers.

The three of them exchanged glances with one another.

"What are you doing?" Clara asked.

"I have something to say," Ed countered.

They both looked at Christian who grabbed Tori by the arm and pulled her to her feet. "We have something to say."

Sam, Tori's nephew, pulled on hem of her shirt. "Are you going to tell them all about the baby now?" he asked innocently, but the room bust into a thunderous roar of commotion and words.

Courtney grabbed for Tyler's hand and gave it a squeeze. He could see the tears ready to spill down her cheeks.

"I didn't see that coming," he whispered to her.

"I did. I could hear it in her voice. That's wonderful news after they lost their other baby."

Deflated, Tyler sat back in his chair. He didn't know about the other baby. What else had he missed during his solitude from his family?

Once everyone managed around the cramped table and hugged Tori and Christian, Clara tapped her knife to her water glass and tugged her husband up next to her.

"Are you all done smothering my brother and his wife?" She tried to make her tone harsh, but Tyler knew better. It might have been the enormous grin on Warner's face that gave it away. "Now, if you don't mind making your way to this side of the table I'd like all of that love and congratulations you just showered on them."

Tyler's Aunt Madeline looked across the table at his cousin. "Clara?"

"Well, heck. I'd wanted to be the life of the party, but we don't do things like that here do we? Yes, Warner and I are also having a baby."

The chaos kicked back up and the room now shifted with people.

Courtney lifted her napkin to her eyes and dabbed away the tears that streamed down her cheeks.

"I knew that one too."

"How did you know that?" Tyler asked amused.

"I could hear it in their voices when he came up the walk and escorted me inside."

"You could make a living reading people."

"Well then," she kissed his cheek. "Get ready for the next."

"Okay, okay!" Ed said quieting down the group that now gathered around his sister and her husband. "I have spent my life being upstaged by both of you. I couldn't hit a damn baseball to save my life. I couldn't catch one either. But Chris could. And I'll be damned if I can sing a note. But my sister gets a recording contract and runs off to Vegas to marry a musician."

Clara kissed Warner and pulled him close.

Ed shook his head. "Well, I'm done being out done by you both." Darcy stood up next to him, their fingers intertwined. "Darcy and I have put in applications for adoption." The room began to celebrate again, but Ed held his hands up in protest. "Now, we know this takes a long time to process. However, sometimes if you have the right channels…"

"Oh, God, you're killing me!" Darcy shouted. "I don't know where to begin." Tears poured down her cheeks and she bounced as though she were going to burst with a secret. "Simone put us in touch with a group that facilitates adoptions. As of twenty minutes ago, we just got word that there is a baby due in two weeks and the mother wants us to be his parents."

She let out a squeal as the room erupted for the third time.

Tyler looked at his mother who sat still in her chair, her eyes wide, and her shoulders raising in what looked like great effort to breathe.

"I'll be right back." He pushed back from the table and moved to his mother. "Are you okay?"

"I'm going to be a grandmother," she heaved out the words.

Tyler smiled. "Yes."

She looked up at him. "Grandmother."

"Yes," he laughed. "You're going to be a wonderful grandmother. You and Madeline are going to spoil that baby rotten."

Regan Benson got to her feet and held her son tightly. "I have you back. You're in love. And now I'm going to be a grandmother. Dear, Lord, could I be more blessed?"

CHAPTER 35

*C*ourtney rested her head against Tyler's shoulder as he stroked her bare back in his bed. Making love to him was only a slight perk she decided, when she thought about this new love.

Knowing Tyler, she'd expected to like his family. But to be swept in with their acceptance and love, that sent her healing to a new level. She'd been quick to accept their invitation for the next weekend as well. Courtney was very sure she'd never want to miss a Sunday dinner with his family.

She'd thought about Fitz all night. Each time Spencer told her something that was supposed to embarrass Tyler, she thought of Fitz. When Avery told her that she enjoyed painting and then invited her to see her work—and then tripped on her apology when she'd realized what she'd said, Fitz would do that too.

But the most amazing part of the evening had been being privy to all of the wonderful announcements that had flooded the house that night. Three siblings. Three babies.

Tyler brushed Courtney's hair from her forehead. "What are you thinking?"

"You're going to be an uncle."

He chuckled. "I am. She looked happy too."

Courtney rolled in closer to him, draping her arm over his bare chest.

"Do you think Ed was being dramatic and only telling everyone about the one baby?"

She felt him shift and knew he was looking down at her now. "One baby?"

Courtney pressed a kiss to his skin. "I assume by next week there will be more announcements. Maybe they don't know yet."

"Are you saying Darcy is pregnant?"

"That's what I'm saying, but she didn't. Not yet."

She felt his breath escape and his chest move as he sucked in more air. "What makes you say that? How do you know that?"

Courtney ran her hand over his chest, letting her fingers linger in the small tuft of hair there. "She didn't feel right, that came across in her voice. There was also this—I don't know—energy to her. I can only assume she was glowing. I felt it."

"If she comes back and says she's having a baby, I'm taking you on the road and we're going to make money with your psychic ability."

She rolled onto her back. "Fitz used to laugh at me, but he never doubted me. If I said something was going to happen, he knew to watch out for it."

Tyler rolled to his side and draped his arm over her. "Did you know he was going to die?"

Courtney bit down on her lip. "I didn't want to know that so I think I fought it. But a little bit of me knew."

"I'm sorry."

"You have to assume that if someone you love is fighting in combat, there is that chance."

"But did you know?"

Courtney felt the tremble start deep in her core until it worked its way to the surface and started her hands shaking.

She clenched them tight. "I knew nearly the moment it

happened, from what I've learned. I woke up and screamed for him."

"There's something else. What is it?"

She turned her face toward his. "I don't know. I mean they said he was killed in combat, but that doesn't feel right."

"What do you think?"

"I don't know. If he were sick, they would have said sick. If it had been an accident, they would have said that."

"What else is there?"

"I don't know. I have to accept I'm not always right."

His lips grazed her forehead. "And Darcy and Ed?"

She laughed easily as she moved in closer to him and his arm pulled her to him tighter. "Oh, I think I'm right there. They are about to have two babies. A gift from another and a gift shared between them."

"I'm looking forward to next week's dinner," he said easily.

So was she, she thought.

REST SHOULD HAVE COME EASILY, but Courtney fought the insomnia in every way she could think of. But no number of sheep she counted was enough. No multiplication table was too hard. No amount of yoga breathing could put her soundly to sleep next to Tyler.

Her mind was filled with the what-ifs of Fitz's death. What if a sniper got him? What if that was all there was to it? Why did she feel like there was a missing piece?

She rolled to her side. She knew why. Because she and Fitz were open to each other about everything—everything except his military career and what he couldn't tell her.

There never should have been something they couldn't say to each other—but she understood it. What she didn't understand was his need to enlist and fight wars she didn't understand. Didn't they have their own wars to fight right there in Nashville?

There was a financial company lingering now that the heir had died. The fortune, no matter what it might be, would eventually fall to her, but the company—well, she could never run that.

And what did she care? She hated math and finances. There were some jobs a sighted person might be best at. That was one of them.

Tyler was turned away from her. She couldn't feel his breath on her neck. If she were in her own home she'd get up and write something, or do something. But as a stranger in his home, she didn't dare go wandering around.

So, she lay there and thought of Fitz. What would he think of Tyler? What would he have done with Fitzgerald Financial? What would he think of her writing stories of survivors for Simone's organization?

The many questions in her head didn't dull the buzzing that kept her awake. Not until she felt Tyler's body roll toward her and his lips press to the back of her neck, did her muscles start to release.

Ed and Darcy were pregnant—this she was sure. Tyler loved her and there was a feeling deep in her gut that said this was forever, even if she was cautious now. But no matter how much she wanted to believe that Fitz had been ambushed and killed, something still nagged at her. When would she be able to let that go?

CHAPTER 36

$\mathcal{A}$very sat with Courtney at a table in an available conference room at Benson, Benson, and Hart. Tyler figured if he had a team working on the gala for *Diamond Gift*, they'd need some room to spread out. Nepotism had certainly played a part in his decision. When he'd asked for space, his father made sure it was available. Next to Tyler's mother and grandmother, Simone was the most important woman in his father's life.

They'd been friends since childhood. It was funny to Tyler that his aunt Simone had known his father longer than anyone. When he was younger, he'd once thought they were brother and sister. They interacted with each other as he and Spencer did. Now he understood relationships—even non-romantic ones.

Avery and Courtney had their heads together discussing catering. Simone had sent Tyler sixteen different emails, which he was dealing with at the moment. The cell phone designated to them for the gala kept ringing, and all the while he'd watch Courtney and notice she was smiling.

This gave her purpose and she was enjoying it far more than

he was at the moment. It might not be assembling a building, but he sure was busy arranging just as many people and jobs.

The room stilled when there was a knock at the door. When Tyler looked up Duane Field stood in the doorway.

"Hello, sir." Tyler quickly got to his feet and moved to the man who stood very large and stiff looking back at him.

Courtney rose as well. He hadn't even spoken, but she knew who was standing there. She certainly had an uncanny gift.

"Tyler," Duane gave him a curt nod.

"It's nice to see you. Please come in. We're kinda spread out, but there is a chair..."

"I've just come for Courtney."

Courtney moved around the table, her hands on each chair guiding her toward her father.

"I'm sorry. I forgot about meeting today."

"Your mother said you were here. The receptionist out front showed me to the room."

Courtney nodded and turned her head toward Tyler. "If you don't mind, I'll see you tomorrow."

"That'll be fine," Tyler said, his voice tense. "I'd be happy to pick you up."

"Thank you. That would be nice." She smiled at him and reached for her father's arm. "Goodbye, Avery. I'll see you tomorrow."

"Good-bye," Avery called back as Courtney walked out of the room with her father.

Avery exchanged glances with Tyler.

"That was tense," she said.

"Yep."

"She didn't even kiss you goodbye."

As strange as it was, that part hadn't fazed him. He'd expected her to be that way around her father when she was at the funeral. But to think that this was the normal way of life for her didn't sit well with him. Courtney was too much of a free spirit to be belittled by just the way the man said her name.

Avery tapped her pen against the table and bit down on her lip. "You don't think she was abused do you?"

"Courtney?" The very suggestion was shocking to him. "No. I don't think that."

"It's just I've seen women jump like that for men who abuse them. I've been around that my whole life with the work my mom has done."

Tyler shook his head. "No. I don't think that at all. I just think that he's over protective of her."

"Because she's blind?"

He tucked his hands into his front pockets and rocked back on his heels. "Yeah."

"My grandfather talks to my mother like that," Avery said sitting back in her seat. "It's as if no matter what she's done in her life, or no matter how many lives she's changed, he wants to make sure she knows she's beneath him."

"That would be why she never went back to Paris?"

Avery nodded. "He doesn't talk to me like that though. He's very considerate where I'm concerned."

"You're his only granddaughter. Maybe that means something to him."

"Maybe. And maybe Courtney's father will begin to ease up on her when the pain of losing his son is over."

Tyler thought about Courtney's father—and the fact that he wasn't her birth father. He wondered, because it was normal to do so, if that had anything to do with how he treated her.

Pulling his hands from his pockets, he rested them on the back of one of the boardroom chairs. "Okay, well, let's get back to work. I want to have the catering menu finalized before we leave tonight."

Avery pulled her hair back in her hands then let it drop down her back. "Will you at least feed me before we work all afternoon? I had a piece of toast for breakfast. I could really use something more substantial."

Tyler laughed. "Of course. Chinese or Italian?"

"Oh, I only want a hot dog from the cart in the square."

"Oh, good. You're a cheap date. Why haven't you been scooped up by a man yet?"

"Because I call the shots and too many men can't handle that."

Tyler grinned at his cousin as she stood from her seat and walked toward him.

Yes, it was going to take a very special man—a very secure man—to love Avery Keller.

CHAPTER 37

*C*ourtney sat in her father's car with her hands clutching her purse on her lap. Her father hadn't said a word to her for almost twenty minutes, which meant he was headed home with her.

"When they get Fitz's headstone up, I'd like to go out and plant flowers," she said trying to ease the tension between them.

"We will make it a point to do that."

"His birthday is next month. I think we should have dinner—a big dinner. Cook steaks and potatoes, just like he'd have wanted. Maybe I could even bake a cake."

"Let's see how your mother is doing by then. She's had a hard week of it. You haven't been around much."

Ah! This was a buffer talk before her mother became emotional on her. Considerate, she thought.

"I spent the day with her last week clearing out Fitz's things." There was tension in her voice, she was sure her father picked up on that.

"She said you had Tyler over. That he'd spent the night."

Courtney kept still, but took a moment to collect her

thoughts. "He was there, yes. He was there through the night, yes. But she thinks he slept over, that's not exactly correct."

She heard her father's large body shift uncomfortably in his seat and then he cleared his throat. "Do you want to elaborate?"

"Daddy," she said knowing it would ease him back down. "I didn't want to get rid of everything that was Fitz's. There was no need to pack him away the day after we buried him. I asked Tyler to come over and help me find a few things. Nothing anyone would miss. But I needed his eyes."

"You just met him."

"I know. But you have to know, there are just some people you meet that make everything okay. They are good people, and Tyler Benson is one of those people."

"So he just came over to help you?"

"Yes. I called him in the middle of the night and he came right over. Daddy, I really like him. He's a good man."

The car slowed and she felt him pull to the right. He was stopping the car.

"Listen, before we get home, I want to talk to you about this man. I've looked him up. I believe you when you say he's not a gold digger."

"Good, because he's not. He gave up a job in his father's business just to work for a non-profit. Gold diggers don't do that."

"I agree." She heard him smack his lips together, which he did when he was deep in thought. "His family seems strong. His aunt is a Pierpont and has the non-profit."

"Correct. She's the heir to Pierpont Oil. Or was."

"His uncle is a doctor and his other uncle a teacher. His father is the CEO of an enormous corporation. There wasn't anything to say he didn't come from good stock."

"I know that, Daddy."

"What do you know about his mother?"

Courtney swallowed hard. "She's a very nice woman."

"She was engaged once."

"Oh," she said and let her voice trail. "Well, he does have a sister he's only known for a few years. She'd given her up at birth."

Her father let out a low hum. "Did you know his mother killed an ex-lover?"

The muscles in her neck stiffened. She'd never lied to her father before. She wasn't going to lie now. "No."

"It was dropped in the press pretty quickly, from what I gathered."

"Press? How hard did you really have to dig for that?" She knew better than that.

"I worry about you."

"How do you know this, Daddy?"

He tapped his fingers against the steering wheel. "I have my connections. You know that. The point is I worry about you and the people you spend your time with. I need to be able to tell your mother who you're with."

The emphasis didn't make her nerves calm any.

"Anyway, it was said to be in self-defense. His cousin Clara was involved and his aunt Arianna. The theater his aunt owns was destroyed by fire and that was where this man's body was found."

Courtney felt a bead of sweat roll down her neck. "Who was the man?"

"Michael Hamilton."

"How do you know this was his mother's lover?"

"I'm going to give it the benefit of the doubt—old ex-lover. They are tied together in items going back nearly twenty-six or more years. He was some investor in L.A. and she worked in a law office that represented him."

She nodded. "And when did he die?"

"After Tyler was born."

Courtney lifted her hand to her trembling lips. "Why are you telling me all of this?"

"So that you know who this man is. Everyone has skeletons in their closets, Courtney. His closet has murder and arson."

CHAPTER 38

*A*very went home by five o'clock, but Tyler sat in the quiet boardroom and stared at his phone.

No need to pick me up. I'll meet you there tomorrow. Goodnight.

The text message had him a bit perplexed and worried. He'd hoped that after she'd spent the afternoon with her father, she'd spend the night with him.

"You still working in here?"

Tyler turned at the sound of his father's voice. "All done for today. Thanks for letting us use the space," he said as he stood from his chair.

"All yours as long as you need it. I've told Simone for years she could have an office here. But she says it gives the wrong impression."

Tyler laughed thinking of his aunt's office. "When three people are working on a project, it's necessary."

Zach Benson, with his cap of nearly white hair, rested his hands on the back of the nearest chair. "So, Courtney..." He let it linger in the air. "She's a nice girl."

"She is."

"Seems to be handling her brother's death well too."

"I think it'll hit her soon. Right now she's doing the brave thing and going on."

"Are you ready for it when she does decide she needs to deal with it?"

Tyler bit down on his lip. "I am. They were very close. Something is going to trigger the emotions. You never know what it's going to be."

His father pulled out the chair he'd had his hands rested on and sat down. Tyler followed, realizing his father needed to talk.

"It might not be the same, but your mother would have things that set her off—about Darcy. When her birthday would pass or she'd see a little girl in just the right dress."

"She'd get emotional about it?"

His father nodded. "She'd never let you or Spencer see that though, but it was there."

"I suppose it was as if she'd lost Darcy the same way Courtney lost Fitz—her brother," he added. "Unexpectedly."

"I can't imagine what it took for her to give Darcy away. She loved Darcy's father. She looked forward to her birth, and she never expected what came of it."

Tyler rubbed his palms on the legs of his pants. He'd known of the man his mother once was engaged to, but he'd only learned of him when Darcy's maternity had come to light. It had been one of the many reasons he'd had to leave and find himself.

"Did it bother you to know she loved someone like him?" Tyler had to know what his father felt.

His father tapped his fingers on the table. "When I fell in love with her, I didn't know any more than she'd been hurt by someone. I didn't know it was physical." He sat back in his chair. "She wouldn't let me in emotionally. But I charmed her," he said, grinning.

"When you found out about Darcy—the baby—did that change how you felt?"

His father shook his head. "No. It changed how your mother dealt with me. Not how I felt about her."

"How did she deal with it?"

"She ran away," he said very matter-of-factly.

Tyler dropped his shoulders and let the similarity in their actions squeeze at him. No wonder his mother had always been so easy on him. He'd caused her a world of hurt, but she'd always let him have his space. Then again, he didn't let many people know where he was while he was running.

"When did she come back to you?"

"She didn't." His father pushed his fingers through his hair and laced his hands behind his head. "I chased her down. I kept coming back and Uncle Carlos would turn me away as nicely as he could. Grandma would pat my face and tell me when she was ready, she'd come to me. I conned her into going out to the house."

"That's where you proposed to her. That I remember."

Zach smiled and leaned forward, resting his arms on the table. "I couldn't let her go. It didn't matter what happened before me. I loved her. That's what mattered."

Tyler swallowed hard. "I think I feel that way about Courtney."

"That's quite a thing to say about someone you've only known a week."

Tyler had never cared for heart to heart talks like these with his father. Zach Benson tended to rationalize things too much. Perhaps it was that analytical brain that made someone so successful at planning out massive building sites.

"I don't have a lot of experience in this department," Tyler admitted. "But everything is different now that I know her. I see the world differently. She taught me that."

His father smiled. "Courtney, who can't see, taught you to see the world differently?"

On a breath, Tyler smiled. "Yes. I can't imagine anything could come my way now that I wouldn't be able to handle."

His father reached toward him and patted his hand. "I think you tumbled into love. That makes for one lucky man."

Didn't Tyler know that? "I think so too."

Zach looked around the room at the table and the piles of papers. "Because I work with all sorts of creative types of people, I'm going to assume that all of this paperwork actually has purpose scattered around like this."

Tyler let out a snort of a laugh. "Crazy enough, but yes. It's perfectly organized."

"You would have been miserable planning out buildings, wouldn't you?"

"Yes."

"I don't hold it against you. I'm very proud of you for going to your aunt and asking to work with her. What she's built there is no less than an amazing miracle." Zach shook his head and smiled. "I never would have thought that would be where Simone Pierpont would have ended up. See," he said, standing, "love will do strange things to you, like having you give up a fortune to marry a person who loves you."

Tyler thought about Fitzsimons Financial and he wondered what Courtney was worth. Not because he was interested in financial gain, but because she didn't seem pretentious.

Weren't they a pair? Both were heirs to big corporations and they'd rather sit in a borrowed boardroom and plan events for a non-profit.

As his father left the room, Tyler began to pick up the papers which were scattered around. The printouts from Courtney's interviews with women that *Diamond Gift* had touched were amazing. She'd been working on a program for the event. It was just what he'd wanted.

Courtney had a gift. She could make people tell her things, and give her permission to share them. Most of it was done over email, some by phone. He couldn't help but wonder, if some of the women saw her, would things be different? Would they have said more or less knowing what Courtney dealt with every day?

Tyler sat down in one of the chairs and kicked his feet up onto the table, now that the office had cleared out.

It had only been a few hours, but he was missing Courtney.

The text message still had him perplexed. Why so cryptic? Why not call? Why stay away?

Tyler stacked the papers and set them in the box next to him. They'd talk about it tomorrow. Her family probably needed her for the night. He had to remember they were still all in mourning. They needed each other and he was a new fixture in her life —and by anyone else's perspective not a permanent one.

His cell phone buzzed in his pocket. This time it was a text from his brother. *Beer. Patio. BBQ. Your house.* Tyler laughed. That was just what he needed.

TYLER LIT the grill and sat down in one of the chairs on the porch overlooking the back yard. The beer in his hand was cold, the air was hot, and his heart ached as he missed Courtney.

He heard the front door slam and a moment later his brother was standing in front of him, loosening his tie, and opening a beer.

"I got notice today that I have to fly out to Oregon tomorrow. Does anything sound less fun?" Spencer asked as he sat down next to Tyler.

"What's in Oregon?"

"Lumber. Looking at a manufacturer that we could buy out and have under our belt."

"I guess that's good, right?"

Spencer nodded. "Especially with the new business venture I convinced Dad and Ed to take on."

Tyler slid his brother a look. "What's that?"

"Housing development." Spencer lifted his beer in salute.

"BBH is going to build housing developments?"

"Starting in three years we will break ground on one just outside Memphis."

"I didn't think I'd ever see that happen."

"That's because you don't give a crap about all of this."

Tyler took a pull from his beer. His brother was right. His focus was on putting together a gala that would bring enough revenue to the *Diamond Gift* and in turn help more women out of bad situations.

"So," Spencer pulled the tie off his neck, "tell me about Courtney. She seemed nice."

"She's more than nice."

Spencer smiled. "Mom said you had it bad for her."

"She said that?"

Spencer nodded as he drank from his bottle. "Said she figured this would be her new daughter-in-law."

The heat on the porch kicked up and Tyler wiped the back of his hand across his brow. "Sure, we're serious. I mean we've said things…"

"Are you kidding me?" Spencer planted his feet on the floor and sat forward to study his brother. "Said things? Like *I love you* kinds of things?"

"Yeah."

"Man, you've known her a week. You don't say stuff like that to a woman you just met."

"Why not?"

Spencer groaned and leaned back in his chair. "It makes you a freaking wuss, that's why."

As if his brother had any room to talk in his prissy button up suit shirt.

"There's a connection, okay? I wouldn't expect you to understand. You're not like me."

"You're right. I'd rather date a lot of women. I'm young. I'm good looking. I'm not going to tie myself down."

They were different, he and his brother. Spencer had always been more carefree, and Tyler more the caretaker. Maybe that came from being the oldest, he didn't know.

"But in all seriousness, man," Spencer looked at Tyler and gave him a nod. "I'm really sorry to hear about her brother." He lifted his beer again in salute. "To our service men and women."

Tyler smiled and lifted his bottle too. Something told him that Fitz Field was one hell of a man, and he'd have liked to have known him.

CHAPTER 39

*C*ourtney had ignored Tyler's text message telling her goodnight.

She needed to be alone tonight with her computer and the internet. She needed to find out who this man was that held her heart so tight.

Sitting quietly through dinner, while her mother sobbed, had been heart wrenching enough. Hearing about the cards and phone calls that still came in with condolences had drained her. When Courtney returned home, after arguing with her mother about staying at their house, she'd collapsed into a chair and cried.

Now she went searching for answers on who Regan Keller was before she married Zach Benson. Really, she couldn't be so cold as to have killed a man.

Her computer read story after story about Michael Hamilton and his marriage to a wealthy debutante. She found connection to Michael Hamilton and Pierpont Oil, which she thought was interesting. It had been three hours of searching before she came to an article that even mentioned Regan Keller and Michael Hamilton together—and it was very brief.

Then she found the article about the fire at the Rockwell Theater. It had been gutted after an extensive remodel. The play Annie had been in rehearsals, and Clara Keller was the lead.

The article went on to say that Regan Benson, Arianna Keller, and Clara Keller had all been treated for smoke inhalation and subsequent injuries. And then it mentioned the body.

The body of an unidentified man was also found inside the theater. There was evidence he had been shot.

Courtney rubbed her hands along her pant leg. Did her father really know what he was talking about?

She sulked back in her chair. Certainly he wouldn't make something up just to detour her from loving a man.

Her father had said it was in self-defense. None of the articles that came up even mentioned Tyler's mother as a suspect. She had to assume his source, most possibly police related, knew what they were talking about.

The point was, Regan Benson, mother of the man she loved, hadn't been pegged as a killer by her own father. So what happened that she'd give up her baby and kill the man so many years later?

Courtney had to know. She had to know the whole story, and she needed Tyler to tell it to her. When she heard his voice she'd know the truth of it all. At that point she'd make her decision as to whether it was better to have loved and lost—or to fight for her man.

TYLER ARRIVED in the office earlier than he'd planned. What else was he to do when he'd been tossing and turning all night long?

His father's assistant, Mary Ellen, had let him into the board room and started a pot of coffee.

"You don't need to do that. We can handle it," he said as she added coffee grounds to the filter.

"It makes me happy. That's probably why I've been doing it for so long." She laughed and pressed the start button. "Who would have thought so many years would fly by so quickly? My baby is having a baby and Zach's babies are running corporations and non-profits."

"I'm not running anything."

She smiled. "In time." Mary Ellen walked past him and toward the door. "I met Courtney yesterday. She's a lovely girl."

"She is."

"Your dad says you're serious about her."

Now Tyler laughed. "Everyone seems to think so."

"Do you?"

He nodded. "Yeah, I think so too."

"Perhaps it's fate, you working from within BBH. Lots of true love has happened within the walls of these offices." She gave him a wink and walked out of the room.

Ten minutes later she was back in his doorway, but this time Courtney was on her arm.

"Thank you, Mary Ellen," Courtney said.

"My pleasure, sweetheart." She gave Courtney's arm a pat and walked away. "I would have been able to find the room myself. I can smell your cologne." Her voice shook as she spoke.

"That strong, huh?"

"Just something I'm keen to be drawn too."

He was across the room and he wasn't moving toward her, so Courtney walked in. Surely her blunt text, lack of response to his texts, and the rigidness in which she stood there were more than enough reason for his lack of movement

She let her cane open up and she walked toward the table. The chairs behind the table moved and she could feel the air stir as he moved.

"Good morning," he said as he touched her arm and leaned in

to kiss her warmly on the mouth. "I have to say, waking up alone this morning wasn't nearly as much fun."

Courtney pushed back her shoulders. "I'm sorry about that. We can't always be together you know. I mean we still have lives away from each other."

Her words weren't ones she'd practiced, or even meant to use.

Tyler stepped away from her and the press of his fingers on her skin disappeared.

"Right. I know that."

"I'm sorry, Tyler." She let out a sigh. "I don't mean to be so nasty this morning. I got a little worked up yesterday."

"Did something happen with your parents?"

Didn't something always, she thought. "Mom is very emotional."

"To be expected."

Courtney nodded. "She's devastated. I'm devastated," she admitted.

"And your dad?"

"He's worried about me—and you."

"Ah," Tyler sighed. "Should I talk to him? I'm never going to hurt you. I've told you that. In fact, even if this doesn't work out between us I'd still want to be your friend."

"Will you shut the door? I want to talk to you about something. I don't know how this is going to go."

He didn't move right away, and she'd heard the breath he'd taken and held in too long. But then he moved past her and the door shut to her back.

Courtney collapsed her cane, pulled out a chair, and sat down.

"Mary Ellen made us some coffee. Would you like some?" he offered.

"I'd really like a bottle of water if you don't mind."

She heard him move toward the corner of the room where a small refrigerator held waters. The door opened. The bottles shifted. And a moment later he was standing next to her.

"Here you go."

"Thank you," she said as she held out her hand for the bottle. Tyler placed it in her reach and she opened it and took a sip.

He moved the chair next to her and sat down. "Is everything okay? You're making me very nervous."

"I'm nervous. It's wearing off," she joked poorly. "I learned something last night and I don't know what to do with the information."

"Okay, tell me what it is and I'll help you."

Courtney sucked in a breath hoping it would give her courage. It only made her light headed.

"Your mother—tell me about the man before your father."

CHAPTER 40

*T*he air in the room grew thick and Tyler leaned back in his chair. The cushion gave to the pressure of his back and the chair squeaked as it rocked.

"That is a very strange request," he said.

"I know. I'm sorry."

"I don't have a lot of information for you. He's Darcy's birth-father. He tried to kill her and my mother. He left her for dead." His voice was rising. "I can't imagine what you'd want to know about him for."

Courtney's heart pounded in her chest. She didn't like this confrontation. She didn't want to make him go through this, but she had to know.

"What happened to him?"

Tyler moved to her side and the chair moved back. She could hear him pace behind her; feel the breeze as his body moved back and forth.

"Why do you want to know all of this? What does this have to do with anything?"

"My father knows your mother killed this man and it worries him that the ghosts in your closet will hurt me."

The room went silent, and the air grew even thicker.

Tyler's pacing had moved from behind her to around the table. He'd walked away from her.

"Your father is accusing my mother of being some vicious attacker? He's worried she'll hurt you or does he think that something like that is in my blood?"

His voice had raised enough she was now more than uncomfortable in her situation. Why had she done this? Why here? There was no escape if her father was right. She didn't want to think he was, but at the very moment, she was scared.

"No, it's not like that."

"Really? You want to know about my mother killing a man who tried to kill her because your father is worried about you. That's what you're saying. He's worried I will hurt you."

"Tyler, stop." She felt the tears begin to sting.

"You asked the question. You'll get your answer." A chair was pushed into the table, though not slammed, but she knew he was angry and she didn't blame him. "Yes. My mother killed the bastard who tried to kill her and my sister. He beat her and left her for dead, Courtney. Left-her-for-dead."

He paced more and now it was quicker. "Tyler…" she started, feeling the need to reel him in.

"She gave Darcy away. She never even looked at her because it hurt too much. She didn't want the bastard to find her baby and hurt her. Can you even imagine wanting a baby so much and then giving her away?"

The very thought had tears breaking free. "No."

"Dad told me just yesterday that every year on her birthday my mother would get very emotional." His voice began to ease. "I never knew anything was going on. I didn't know she mourned someone so much."

"That says something about her, that she could love that much after someone hurt her so badly."

He stopped moving. "Yeah." She heard him move around the

table and come back to the seat next to her. He pulled it out and sat down.

"My uncle told the man that my mother had died. He'd replaced her with some other woman and that was the reason he'd tried to kill her. But my uncle told him she and the baby died and he went away, which was the plan."

"Why not send him to jail?"

"Because then it drug it out and involved my mother more. My uncle was trying to just make it go away. I don't know. The man moved to Europe and that was better, at the time, than dragging my mother though some battle in court."

Courtney nodded. She supposed she understood that. "He found out she was alive."

Tyler took her hand. "Yes. Though he didn't come after her then. It wasn't until after Spencer and I were born that he'd lost everything and he came back for revenge. He began stalking my aunt Arianna because he'd seen her in New York. Then he stalked Uncle John because he'd become involved with my aunt and would lead him to my dad. He reeled them all in until my aunt and my mom were at the theater together one night alone."

"Clara was with them."

"You sure do know a lot," he said interlacing their fingers. "Wrong place-wrong time."

"He hurt them."

"He knocked out John. Took Clara, hit her, and locked her in a closet before setting the theater on fire."

Courtney covered her mouth with her other hand as the tears fell freely down her cheeks.

"All I know is they got her out of the closet, but the theater was engulfed. Somewhere in the chaos of black and smoke my mother got the gun my aunt carries on her and shot the bastard."

A small unnecessary croak of a laugh escaped Courtney. "She shot him in the dark in an engulfed building?"

She felt the tension ease away from his fingers. "She's quite a marksman. She taught Spencer and me how to shoot. Oh, heck, she taught my dad to shoot."

Now she laughed freely but then brought it back in. The mood was still too serious to enjoy that insight into his mother. "He was going to kill her," she said.

"Her, John, Arianna, and Clara. I know she'd have killed him even if she was going to die, to protect me and my brother."

Courtney gave his hand a squeeze now. "And Darcy."

He rubbed her hand with his other hand. "Yeah, and Darcy even though she had no idea where she was."

"The articles only talk about the fire and a man being found. Not about your mother."

"But you knew that."

"My father has many connections."

She heard him groan. "So does my father. It was swept under the rug to protect us. Yes, she killed a man in self-defense."

Courtney began to sob harder now. "I'm sorry. Oh, I'm so sorry. I shouldn't have worked this into something that it wasn't."

He pulled her to him. "It's okay. I've never dealt with it. I needed to."

"I can't imagine your mother had to go through that." The sobs came harder. "She survived and she found love. She had two more sons. Her daughter came back to her."

"Yes."

"What if had he gotten to her in that fire? What if…"

"She wasn't going to let him. There was no way she was going to leave my brother and me."

And then everything inside of her broke loose. Fitz had left her.

TYLER PULLED her even closer to him as tears poured down her cheeks and her body shook. "Honey, take it easy. Breathe. Breathe."

She sucked in a breath but it was a ragged one. Her entire body quaked against him.

"Fitz," she said between those breaths she tried to draw in. "Fitz."

"Okay, okay." He kissed her forehead. This was the moment he and his father had been talking about. Of all things to have set her off about her brother, he thought.

He let her cry against his chest and he simply held her, stroking her hair. Avery looked in the window by the door and he'd nodded her away for a moment. She knew. She understood, he could see it in her eyes. Right now the moment was for Courtney and he'd hold her as long as he needed to.

The sobs lasted the better part of an hour, but he held her. She clung to him and he gave her comfort. He wiped her tears and kissed her cheeks—and finally it stopped.

"I'm sorry. I'm so sorry."

"Shh," he said wiping away the last of the tears. "It's okay. It's very okay. You needed to do this."

"Not here. Not when I came in here accusing you of being something you're not."

"Now." He pulled her to him again. "And I'm sure it'll come again."

"He left me, Tyler," she said with her face pressed to his chest. "He always promised to stay and be with me. He left me."

"Not on purpose."

She nodded. "I know. Just as your mother wouldn't have left you on purpose either. And she didn't leave Darcy on purpose."

Who would have thought two very different things could be so much alike in feeling?

Courtney's breath began easing, and she back pulled back. "I shouldn't feel so sad that he was defending his country when he died. But I do. I take it very personally that he died and left me here alone. He always promised me he'd come back to me."

"I'm sure you were in his thoughts when he died. I can't imagine you weren't."

"He should have fought harder."

Tyler pulled her to him again. Yes, these tears would come again. She wasn't ready to let Fitz's death go yet.

When Avery happened by the door again, he waved her in. Courtney sat up and wiped her eyes.

"Everything okay in here?" Avery asked as she walked through the door.

"Oh, I'm just having a meltdown," Courtney laughed. "Good thing I don't have to worry about whether my mascara ran down my cheeks."

"I hate when that happens," Avery said.

"My friend put mascara on me once. I have no idea if it looked good or not, but I remember my eyelashes getting stuck together."

Avery let out a hearty laugh. "Yep. Oh, what we do to look beautiful."

Tyler sat back in his chair and looked at Courtney. It was a shame she'd never know how beautiful she was on the outside, but it didn't really seem to matter to her. Even with tear streaked cheeks, no one held a candle to her.

Avery pulled a pile of papers out of the bag she'd carried in with her. "Well, now down to work. We just received RSVPs from four hundred people for the gala."

"Already?" Tyler sat up in his chair. "We didn't even get all of the invites out yet."

She grinned wide at him. "I might have at one time mentioned to a few of our corporate sponsors something about a huge family event."

"You might have?"

She grimaced. "I told you I hate this." She handed him the papers. "It's worth two million to the organization if we can make something family friendly happen."

Tyler felt the blood drain from his head. Hadn't there been enough stress this morning? He rubbed at his temples and let out a breath. Okay, he could do this. He winced at the pain in his chest caused by the stress his cousin had caused. Sure—he could do this.

CHAPTER 41

*I*t had become work, and Tyler had roped Courtney into it much more than getting some information on past recipients. *The Diamond Gift* was having a family extravaganza—thanks to Avery's mention of it.

The entire week had been spent with long hours, late nights, and about a million phone calls between the three of them.

Thanks to the long list of connections that Simone and his father had, they were able keep the venue and expand it out into the parking lot. They would have tents and events outside as well as dancing and entertainment inside.

One thing was for sure, Courtney was not only the most organized person he'd ever known, and Avery the least, but she was brilliant with the ideas.

Avery pulled the pencil, which was holding up her bun, out of her hair. Her hair fell over her shoulders and she shoved it back.

"It is nine o'clock on Friday night and I'm in a board room hashing out details on an event that is two and a half months away."

"Which is three times its normal size," Tyler reminded her.

"And worth three times as much."

He laughed. "Go home. We need to finalize the menu tomorrow."

"Tomorrow? Saturday?"

He tossed a wadded paper in her direction. "Nine o'clock too early?"

"Damn early for a Saturday," she groaned as she stood and gathered her bag. "It's a good thing I respect Courtney or I'd probably kick your ass for making me work so hard."

"I could have taken the job next year and this would have all been yours."

She groaned. "Well played. I'll see you both in the morning."

When Avery had left, Tyler rolled his chair closer to Courtney's. Her fingers were flying on the keys of her computer and her headphones were tucked into her ears so she could hear the words she was typing.

Tyler gently took hold of her wrists and removed her hands from the keyboard.

She laughed as she turned toward him. "Do you need something, Mr. Benson?"

Tyler pulled the ear buds from her ears and laid them atop her keyboard. "There is no one in this whole building," he said brushing her hair over her shoulder.

"You're a liar. There is security. Video recording cameras. And I can hear a vacuum."

"I don't hear that."

"You don't have my superpowers, remember?"

Tyler moved in closer to her resting his hand on her cheek. "My father has a Murphy bed in his office."

Courtney pulled back. "I'm not even going in there, let alone having sex with you in your father's office."

Now he laughed. "If I take you home?"

"Your home."

"Good. You're sensible. It's closer." He moved in and took her mouth with his.

He was feeling a need for her surge through him, but when she opened up to his kiss, he was very sure it surged through her as well.

"We have to go through my dad's office to get the private elevator."

"Fine, but we're not stopping. You can wait till we get home."

"Can you?"

She gave him a firm shove against the chest. "I guess we'll have to see."

THEY HAD MADE IT HOME, barely, before they slammed the front door and took in after each other, tearing off clothes.

Tyler was more than a little happy that he was the only one living in the house. That was rare enough with his family, but at that moment it was an absolute blessing because most of the moaning seemed to be coming from him.

They were a storm of hands and lips as they maneuvered from the front door toward the couch. Tyler managed to kick the end table and then the coffee table warranting a laugh from Courtney.

"Why are you laughing?" he asked with his lips pressed to hers as he pushed her shirt off her shoulders.

"I'm the one who hasn't fallen over anything. You'd never make it in my world." She gave him a shove forcing him onto his back on the couch before she straddled him. "But you'll never feel like I do either."

His fingers pulled at the straps on her bra as she shook her head back letting her hair move behind her.

"What does that mean? I'm obviously feeling a whole lot right now."

She was smiling down at him. "I feel your breath." She pressed her fingers to his lips. "I know your heart beat." Her hands glided down his throat to his chest.

Courtney unclasped the bra that kept her skin from his hands and let it drop off her arm to the floor.

"You have a scar here," she said tracing her finger down his side to the scar over his hip. "You have another on your back at your shoulder blade."

She lowered herself, pressing her bare breasts against his chest. "Your voice rises slightly when you're worried about something and gets deeper when you're on the phone with people."

Pressing her lips to his chest she let her hands roam over his shoulders. "And when I kiss you right here," she moved her lips to his collarbone. "You gasp."

He did just that and then sucked in another breath, giving her hair a tug and bringing her mouth to his. "I know things about your body too."

"Yes, you do." She kissed him. "But you can't make love in the dark without falling into things. I can."

"Well, I guess I'll never match up." He cupped her breasts in his hands sending her upright over him. "I'll just have to make it count."

CHAPTER 42

*T*yler watched Courtney sleep in his arms. Two weeks ago, she'd dropped her scarf and he'd picked it up. The moment she'd held out her hand to take it from him, he was sure that was when he'd fallen in love with her.

Now her skin was pressed to his and he did know her heartbeat.

His cousin Clara and her husband came to mind. They hadn't known each other much longer when they'd run off to Las Vegas and gotten married. Now they were starting a family.

Tyler pressed a kiss to Courtney's head in the darkness of early morning. She wasn't the fly off and get married kind of girl, and he owed his mother more than that. And what did it matter if they got married tomorrow or in four years? This was the woman. She was the right one and his heart knew that even after only two weeks.

Courtney stirred against him. "What time is it?" Her voice was soft.

"Three o'clock."

"You're awake, why?"

Tyler brushed his hand over her shoulder and pulled her closer. "I was watching you sleep."

She moaned against him, perhaps more in protest than with enjoyment. "Why?"

"I want to marry you."

She stilled even more against him and then pushed herself up on her elbow. "You need more sleep. Go to sleep," she said lowering herself back to his chest.

That wasn't going to do. It burned in him now. He rolled her onto her back and leaned in over her. "Not now. Not this month or even this year, but I want to marry you."

"Let's talk about it in the morning. After coffee. I think you need coffee."

He let out a small laugh. "I'm fine. I don't need coffee. I don't need sleep." He sat up and pulled her to sit too. "Do you love me?"

"Yes," she said but it wavered as though she thought he was crazy.

"Between you and me, and no one else, someday will you marry me?"

Courtney was tense and he didn't blame her. Her face was still full of sleep and as she ran her hands over her it he knew she was still trying to comprehend what he was doing.

"Really, we should talk about this…"

"Now." He took her hands in his. "I'm not going to run and tell my family and until I can make one hell of a to- do about it—in time—we wouldn't mention it to your parents either. But, Courtney, someday in the not too distant future would you marry me?"

"Are you crazy?"

"About you, yes."

"You're proposing to me, naked in your bed at three in the morning?"

"Yes."

"I've known you two weeks."

"Long enough."

"But we're not going to tell anyone, yet? This is between you and me?"

He laughed and ended it on a breath, "Yes."

She wasn't answering him as quickly as he'd have liked. Okay, in her defense he'd stumped her while she was still sleepy.

"Courtney..." he reached for her, brushed his hand down her hair. "I didn't mean to..."

"I can't imagine not being your wife."

He held still for a moment. "What does that mean?"

"I've thought about it. I've been thinking about it for two weeks." She gathered his hands in hers. "I'll never see the faces of my children. I'll never know when you've become an old man—well I'll never see it. I may be very independent, but there is a factor that I'll always need something—someone to guide me through my day to day. There is a lot to think about here."

"I know but..."

She pressed her fingers to his lips to stop him. "But, those are fears I've always had. Who could possibly love me enough to take care of me forever? Who would take the time to make sure I know what my children look like? Who would...?"

"I would," he said against her fingers before she lowered them. "I would do all of that because to me it's not a burden."

"I believe that." Her voice trembled now and not because of sleep.

"Then?"

She ran her hands up his arms until they were linked around his neck. She pulled him back to her and eased him down over her. "Then, in time, when we are ready to take that step and tell our parents, I would be honored to marry you, Tyler."

He felt tears burn in his eyes, but he wouldn't let them fall. Not now. "You'll marry me?"

"Yes."

"You glow in the moonlight."

"And you have a bad habit of talking too much," she said as she rolled him over on his back and made love to him—him the happiest man in the world at the moment.

CHAPTER 43

The home that had been Tyler's grandparents' house, and now was Ed and Darcy's home was loud and fragrant, again. It was Sunday, and Tyler had managed to be with his family for the third Sunday in a row. Yes, this was why he'd come home. The chance to fall in love with a beautiful woman was only a bonus.

Ed and Chris were setting up tables on the back lawn when Tyler arrived.

"Did you decide the house was too small?" he joked as he walked out the back door.

"It's warm and beautiful. So we're grilling tonight," Ed responded as he leveled out the table in the grass. "Where's Courtney?"

"I lost her already. It seems as though your wife has some ideas to share with her and Avery about the gala."

Ed laughed. "Girls planning a party. She fits right in."

"Hey," Chris shouted toward him. "Catch." He threw him a can of beer, wet from the cooler.

"Thanks."

Ed and Chris moved toward him. "I remember our dads

standing out here doing this. Full circle, huh?" Tyler noted as Spencer walked out of the house, grabbed his own beer, and joined them.

"And now you all have kids coming."

Ed's eyes flashed wide for a moment and then he smiled. "We met with the birth mother yesterday. The baby is due next week, so really anytime."

"That's crazy," Spencer added his opinion. "Are you ready for that?"

"No," Ed laughed loud. "I'm not. But at the same time I am. I've never been more excited about anything in my life."

Tyler wondered if there was more to it the way something danced in Ed's eyes. Then he thought about Courtney's feeling that they were expecting too. He wondered if the night would grow even more eventful.

COURTNEY HAD a bowl of potato salad, she'd helped Tyler's grandmother make, in her arms. Authentic German potato salad, his grandmother had told her in a deep full, muddled accent.

Darcy had held open the door for her and told her the location and number of steps to walk down.

When she hit the soft grass at the bottom she stopped. She could sense Tyler standing right in front of her.

"You're beautiful," he said softly as he moved in and kissed her on the cheek.

"It's the potato salad."

She heard him breathe in the fragrant whiff. "Grandma made salad?"

"Grandma taught me how to make it."

"I have got to be the luckiest man in the world. A beautiful woman who can make my grandmother's salad. C'mon, I'll show you to the table."

He offered her his elbow and they walked to the table that Ed and Christian had set out in the yard.

Noise was a staple at these dinners, she'd quickly learned. But it was the most pleasant noise she'd ever heard in her life. Dinner at her house was all about her mother talking about herself.

Somewhere between her bite of Grandma's salad and the sip of Madeline's lemonade, Ed had stood and announced that they had an announcement. She grinned and Tyler took her hand and gave it a squeeze.

"As you know Darcy and I will be parents very soon."

"Very soon," Darcy said enthusiastically. "The baby is due anytime. We met the mother and the baby is full and healthy and ready."

"Right. Well, this will be good practice for us." She heard a cell phone ring and Ed cleared his throat. "Yes. When? Where? Um, yes, okay. Twenty minutes."

The crowd which was usually loud was hushed to absolute silence.

"Ed, are you okay?" she heard his father ask.

"Yeah, um, wow."

"Ed, what is it?" Darcy's voice was filled with fear.

"Oh, well, let me finish my announcement. Yeah. Anyway, all of this will be great practice for us because Darcy and I are expecting our own baby as well."

Tyler leaned in to Courtney as the voices of the family raised in congratulations.

"You were right. That superhero power again."

"Hold on. There's more," she whispered to him.

"Um, thanks everyone. But we have to go," Ed's voice was hurried and Courtney heard the folding chair move.

"Ed, what's going on?" Darcy asked, again her voice filled with panic. Courtney heard Ed whisper something. "Oh. Oh! Oh, we have to go. We have to go."

"What happened?" Ed's mother now asked.

"Our baby is on the way. That was the birth mother's mother. They just took her to the hospital."

"Go. Go!" Simone said through tears, obviously moved that she'd helped yet someone else.

There were cheers and sobs filling the air among the breeze rustled song of the leaves in the trees. Courtney felt the stir of emotion begin to take over with Tyler's hand in her own.

She moved in closer to him. "I love your family. You need to know that."

"I know that." He kissed her cheek.

"I want to be part of this," she said as softly near his ear as she could.

"When you're ready we'll make our own announcement then."

She rested her cheek against his. "In time. Today and next week certainly belong to Ed and Darcy."

"Carlos and Madeline just ran out too," Tyler confirmed. "My mother is already in the house. I don't think my father knows what's going on," he said with a chuckle

"I'm thinking this party will be relocating."

"I suppose you're right. That's how we roll here."

"That's because life and family is so important."

"Couldn't have said it better myself." She felt him shift. "There go Warner and Clara." He laughed. "Tori is crying, and the kids are trying to pull her into the house to leave. I think Chris is already in the car."

"Perhaps Uncle Tyler should be there too."

"Uncle Tyler." He sighed—actually sighed. "Hadn't thought about that really. But I'll go later. I think there are going to be a lot of visitors. She won't miss me."

"Then we should help clean up. This house needs to be ready for that new life coming home to it."

~

THE PHONE CALL had come in after Tyler and Courtney had settled in on her sofa.

"I'm an uncle," Tyler pulled Courtney closer to him.

"To a nephew or a niece?"

He chuckled. "Oh, yeah." He kissed her on the forehead. "Her name is Emily."

"After your grandmother."

Tyler stroked her hair. "Yeah. She created the eclectic family and Ed and Darcy consciously added to it with that in mind."

"I think that's beautiful."

"She's completely healthy and they can take her home tomorrow."

"And the birth mother?"

"She's doing fine. She's fourteen."

"Oh, my."

"Yeah. She is very sure she doesn't want to be a mother and she tried to hide the pregnancy until it was too late."

"Small blessings in everything," Courtney added.

"We've been invited over tomorrow. I told them we'd come with Avery at lunch since we have a lot of work to do."

Courtney snuggled in closer to him and Tyler contemplated everything that had happened. He'd never stopped to realize that life moved so fast. In one moment a life could be taken from you or the gift of life could be given.

One moment you're a child—the next you're in charge of your own future.

Clearly now, he thought of the moment at dinner when Courtney said she wanted to be part of his family. Didn't he want that more than anything? It was much too soon to bring it up to her parents, he was sure of that. But he wouldn't dream about announcing it until he'd spoken to her father—asked his approval.

Dear Lord, what would he do if he didn't get it?

"You're thinking awful hard," Courtney said.

"I am. So much has happened in the past few weeks. I was just taking inventory."

"The day Fitz died I thought my heart was so broken it would ever mend." She sat up next to him and turned toward him. "I couldn't have expected that I'd meet you on that plane and my whole life would change."

"Small blessings in everything, just as you said."

She leaned back into him again. "I could have done with having had it all and Fitz here too."

Tyler draped his arm over her shoulders. "I know. But he'd never have left you on purpose."

"No. Nothing could ever make him have done that."

CHAPTER 44

*C*ourtney and Avery had convinced Tyler at lunchtime
that work would need to wait. They wanted to see Ed
and Darcy's new daughter. He'd quickly conceded.

Avery all but pushed them both out of the way when they
walked into Ed and Darcy's house. "I'm holding her first."

Courtney laughed. "You know, she's being silly. She'll hold her
first and look at her. I'll hold her longer and really get to know
her."

Tyler laughed as they walked in.

"Oh, Ed, she's beautiful," Avery was saying when Tyler led
Courtney into the living room.

"She is. She's absolutely perfect," he agreed.

"I was thinking I'd have more time to prepare," Darcy said.
"Two weeks to become a mother, that's not normal."

"I'm sure your mother and father felt the same way," Courtney
said and then wondered if she should have.

The room was silent for a moment. "You're right. You know, I
remember my mother saying that. They'd waited years for a baby
and then one day they got a phone call that there was a baby and
they could come and get her." Courtney felt Darcy's hand on her

arm. "Thank you for reminding me that I was someone's miracle too."

The tension in the room subsided. Darcy walked Courtney through the nursery they had put together so quickly.

"The bassinette is one that has been in the Keller family for years. Curtis slept in it. Ed, Chris, and Clara. And of course Tyler and Spencer. I suppose it's going to be a very busy bed here soon," Darcy said softly.

"Does it bother you to all be having babies at the same time?"

"Oh no," she said very quickly. "What a blessing. My sisters and I will have a lot in common, don't you think? We can go out and eat strange things. We can complain about this and that together. And in the end we can hold and coo over our own babies because none of us will be fighting to hold the other's baby."

Courtney laughed. "Sounds like it's all worked out."

"And you and Tyler?"

"What about us?" she asked and her voice fluttered a bit.

"I know you haven't known each other long, but you're very serious."

Courtney swallowed hard. "We are. There is a lot of excitement and a lot of mourning going on around us right now. We need to take some time to figure it all out."

Darcy rested her hand on Courtney's arm again. "I'm so sorry about your brother."

"Thank you. It hits hard when I'm least expecting it."

"C'mon, time for Avery to give up the baby," Darcy laughed and escorted Courtney back down the steps.

TYLER WOULD ADMIT he wasn't one for holding babies. In fact, other than Spencer, and he himself was not more than a baby, he didn't remember ever holding one.

But when Courtney came back into the room that was what

he was doing. He was holding his niece, and he could have sworn she smiled at him.

"Come sit by me. I have Emily."

He reached a hand up to guide her down next to him.

"Are you ready for her?" he asked.

"I'm nervous. I haven't held too many babies."

"Me neither, but she seems content. I'm going to lay her in your arms."

Courtney held her arms to accept the baby and Tyler slid Emily into them.

"Oh, my. This is wonderful," Courtney said holding back the tears that were forming. "Tell me what she looks like," she said as she let Emily wrap her little hand around her finger.

"She's dark like Ed," Darcy said. "Ed is half Puerto Rican and half Italian. Emily is Hispanic."

"You truly have continued the eclectic mix of your family."

"That was our plan," Ed said.

"She has a full head of black hair," Darcy continued and Courtney smoothed her hand over Emily's head.

"It'll be curly too. In time," Courtney said.

"How do you know that?"

Tyler laughed. "She has these superpowers like that. You don't want to second-guess her. She knew you were pregnant when you hadn't announced it yet."

"You did?" Darcy laughed.

"I can see the things others can't," she said with a brilliant smile as Emily cuddled closer to her.

Tyler draped his arm over her shoulders and looked down at that new eclectic addition to the Keller family. This baby would never know anything but love and compassion. That's how the family worked. And as Courtney cooed to the baby and felt her with delicate hands, Tyler knew that Courtney, with her superpowers, belonged here too.

CHAPTER 45

*P*lanning, negotiating, replanning, and late nights became the norm for the next two months. But the team of Tyler, Avery, and Courtney had pulled it off. The event was a mere two weeks away, and Tyler was pleased with what they'd done in such a short amount of time.

He worked at Courtney's desk, in the corner of her living room, while she prepared dinner for him. Piece by piece, his life had been slowly moved into her house and only unimportant items remained in his house for the time being. When they announced their engagement, then he would move in completely.

They'd discussed it. It made sense for her to live where she knew the layout the best. Though, in time, when they had their own family, that would have to change. Neither of their houses were big enough for more than one child. At least that's what Tyler thought since he'd had ample room to run and play.

Courtney had been a little edgy the past two weeks dealing with her mother, and Tyler thought that was acceptable. After all, Fitz's birthday had passed, the headstone had been erected, and her mother had fallen apart on more than one occasion while

Courtney had been the rock to settle her. And Tyler had been there after to settle Courtney.

What had surprised him most was the lack of people who contacted Courtney to see if she was okay since Fitz's death. She loved him so, but didn't the rest of the world? He couldn't think of a single time her phone had rang and someone had said, "I'm calling to see how you're feeling."

He thought better of that. His own mother had called her nearly every week to do that.

Pride swelled in him. That's what she needed more than anything at this point. She needed to be his wife and an official part of his family.

Tomorrow. He would go to her father tomorrow and ask for her hand in marriage. He'd propose at the gala. Yes, that would be the perfect venue to make it official. Of course, he'd keep it under his hat and not make a scene. But this had brought them together. It had let Courtney shine as a writer and a planner of big things. She might not see the world the way he did, but she saw a bigger picture, that was for sure.

"Dinner is ready," Courtney's voice broke the silence he was sitting in.

She stood in the doorway, a vision of beauty in an apron.

"Smells wonderful."

"You're a man. It's food. Of course it's wonderful." She laughed easily.

Tyler stood and moved to her swiftly. He gathered her in his arms and pressed a kiss to her lips. "I love you."

"Those are big words for a simple meal."

"It's not the meal. It's so much more."

She held her hands to his chest. "I love you too. Now let's eat before it gets cold."

Courtney turned out of his arms and went back into the kitchen.

Oh, in two weeks she'd understand the extent of those

words and then for the rest of her life he'd make sure to fully show her. Throughout his life, he'd seen his parents. They never faltered in their love. They never distrusted the other one. Sure, there had been arguments and tears, and in the end hugs and kisses.

Courtney Field deserved that for the rest of her life, or the rest of his at least.

He sat down at the table across from where she sat. He thought, this was to be the norm—dinner with the most beautiful woman on the planet—forever.

∼

COURTNEY and her mother were going to go shopping. Tyler had to give her credit. She was doing everything she could to ease her mother's pain

Tyler had called Courtney's father, and Duane Field had invited him over.

He was sure he'd much rather have met the man in public. If what Tyler had to say upset her father, who knew what he was capable of doing.

Tyler pulled up in front of the house he'd been to a few times since the reception after Fitz's funeral. As he walked up the front steps, and held his finger out for the doorbell he heard his name being called from the garage.

He stepped off the porch and followed the noises around to the side door of the massive garage where he found Duane Field with the barrel of a shotgun in his hand and a rag.

Tyler couldn't help but think of the Rodney Atkins song about the dad cleaning his gun when boys came to call on his daughter. He wondered if this was some kind of similar maneuver.

"Mr. Field, thank you for meeting with me."

Duane Field gave a grunt. "I figure you've come out here man to man since you've never come alone before."

The garage was very warm, but Tyler didn't fidget, that would certainly come across as weak.

"I have."

"Do you shoot?"

"Yes, sir. My mother was a champion marksman. She taught me well."

He saw it flash in the man's eyes, the comment about his mother and a gun, but he didn't say anything else.

"C'mon. I have a trap set up out back. Let's see if any of that wore off on you."

Tyler smiled and nodded nervously. It was Tennessee after all. He couldn't be the only man who showed up to ask the blessing of a man to marry his daughter and a gun was involved.

He followed Duane Field around the garage and out into the field where he had, in fact, set up a range with a trap and boxes of clay pigeons.

"Can you Skeet shoot?" he asked, turning toward Tyler.

"I can."

And that was all it took to have Duane Field hand him a gun and set forth to have him prove that he could in fact shoot skeet along side a man of distinguished military honor.

After two hours, Tyler's shoulder was numb. And most assuredly, there'd be a huge bruise there tomorrow. But the smile that very nearly crept onto Duane Field's face was worth his own pain.

"C'mon. Maria has some lemonade on the porch for us," Duane said as he led Tyler around the back of the house.

When they approached the house, Maria walked out of the kitchen with a tray of lemonade over ice and a pitcher to fill from.

Duane motioned for Tyler to sit. When he did, he winced from the pain in his shoulder and Duane laughed.

"Gets ya every time, doesn't it?"

"I haven't shot in a long time," Tyler admitted.

"You did a lot of traveling, I understand."

"Yes. Took a few years to find myself. Worked in different places around the world."

"A man needs to do that. Military did that for me."

Tyler hadn't thought they'd have been on the same level with that, but perhaps it would make it easier now.

"Let's get down to it," Duane continued. "Why are you here?"

Now Tyler felt the sweat bead up on his neck and the air grow so thick he thought he'd choke.

"Sir, I know I haven't known your daughter very long. And I realize that circumstances in which we met were a bit odd. But," he reached into his pocket and pulled out the ring box he carried with him. "I'd like to ask her to marry me."

He opened the box to show her father the solitaire he'd picked out with Avery to present to Courtney.

Duane Field took it from him and studied it, silently. After a long moment he handed it back.

"What makes you think she'll marry you?"

"We've discussed it."

"So this is already done? You're here to show off your manners?"

Now Tyler's palms were sweaty too. "Sir, I think it is very important to have the family's blessing for such things. We have discussed getting married, but I'd like to propose to her and make it very special."

"When do you want to do this?"

"At the *Diamond Gift* gala, sir."

Duane Field nodded slowly. "Her mother mentioned that we were attending."

"Yes."

"Courtney isn't going to be the easiest wife, you know. She will always need someone to watch after her."

"Sir, I'm aware of the limitations she has, but I also see the fierce independence she has as well. I don't see her blindness as any kind of curse, and neither does she."

"Fitz did," he said very sternly.

"I'm sorry he felt that way. I know he felt some guilt over it. But she doesn't see it like that. And her blindness doesn't affect me and it does little to detour her."

"Children. How will she care for children?"

"I think she'll care for them just fine. She does remarkably wonderful around my niece."

Duane Field nodded slowly. "You've only known her a few months. How can you make a lifetime worth of assumption in a few months?"

"With all due respect, sir, I think I knew in the first week this is what I wanted. I love your daughter very much."

Courtney's father picked up a glass of lemonade and sipped it slow, keeping a steady eye on Tyler the entire time.

"A lesser man would have bought her a gold band since she can't see the shimmer and beauty in the one you showed me."

"She sees more than we do. She's certainly taught me that."

Duane Field stood and Tyler followed. It was now that he realized what an enormous stature he had and how small and weak Tyler must look to him.

Courtney's father held out his hand to Tyler. "It takes quite a man to see those qualities in a woman, sighted or not. You have my blessing."

Tyler shook Duane Field's hand and hoped that he wasn't too zealous or nervous when he thanked him sincerely for everything.

CHAPTER 46

*C*ourtney couldn't remember the last time she and her mother had laughed so much. They'd had brunch and Courtney might have had one too many mimosas.

Her mother insisted on going shopping for new dresses to wear to the gala. Because she was having so much fun, Courtney had agreed.

"I think that looks lovely on you," her mother said as Courtney stepped out of the fitting room.

"I like how it feels," she said running her hands down over the skirt. "Tell me about it."

"It's lovely. There are a lot of festive colors. The main color is turquoise with splashes of yellows, oranges, purples, white, and reds."

"Oh, my. That sounds very loud."

"But that's the thing. It's not. It's so beautiful and the colors against your skin…" Her words cut off. "Oh, honey. It's just beautiful."

Courtney figured that if her mother was emotionally moved by the dress, then it must look fantastic. She couldn't wait for

Tyler to see it. She placed her hand on her chest and felt the neckline. She liked that, too.

"It's settled then. This is the dress."

"Oh, Courtney, Tyler is going to love it," her mother said the thrilling buzz that went through her when her mother actually acknowledged him.

Courtney had been very careful to not talk about him too much outside the realm of the gala, but there must have been something that spoke volumes to her mother.

Her mother searched for a dress for herself, though her mother didn't seem as easy to please.

"I'm worried I won't look right," she said after the fourth dress."

"What do you mean?"

"Well, this is a big thing. I mean, I've seen it in the news for years. There are some very elite names there."

"Yes, that's how the organization makes their money."

"I know. I just want to look right."

Courtney reached out her hand to touch her mother. "You will look just fine. Trust me. The people you are going to meet are very welcoming and accepting. You never could look wrong to them."

"If they are anything like Tyler, I'm sure they will be very nice."

Courtney smiled. "You like him? Really?"

"Oh, of course I do, honey. I think he's a very nice young man."

"What if I told you I could see spending my life with him?"

The room was quiet. Courtney had hit a nerve. "Well, that is a very long way away. Perhaps we could talk about that some other time. I'll try on that blue dress. I did kind of like it best," her mother said leaving her alone."

It wasn't so far away, she wanted to tell her. There was a spike of emotion taking over. What had she really expected? She needed to be grateful enough that her mother liked him, perhaps when she met the whole family, she'd understand how amazing they all really were.

COURTNEY TRIED NOT to let the single little thing her mother said upset her, but it was hard. That was until she walked through the front door of her house and smelled the aroma of grilled steaks and baked potatoes.

Of course her mother had insisted on walking her inside. She wondered how this might go.

"Who is here?" she asked the moment they walked in the door.

"Who do you think, Mother."

"You're home," Tyler called from the kitchen and a moment later she felt him in the same room. "Oh, hello, Mrs. Field."

"Tyler."

"It's very nice to see you see you." He moved in, wrapped his arm around Courtney's waist and kissed her softly on the cheek. "How was your day of shopping?"

"It was wonderful," her mother said. "I bought Courtney a beautiful dress for the gala, since it's less formal than in the past."

Courtney felt the sting of her words, perhaps Tyler didn't.

"Yes, it'll be family friendly and I think an enormous success," he said and Courtney had to admit she loved how he handled things. "Courtney has written some amazing pieces for the media and for our event specific press kits."

"She always was good at dabbling in writing. Though nothing serious."

Courtney's body tensed.

"Oh, I don't know," Tyler intercepted her mother's comment. "I've read many of her things, and she's got some amazing talent. When the gala is over, and we have some breathing room, my cousin's husband Warner said he knew a few people who could look at her work. It's very promising." He gave her a squeeze to let her know he was on her side. "I've grilled some steaks and potatoes. Would you be able to join us, Mrs. Field?"

Courtney wondered what he was doing. She certainly wasn't in the mood for her mother any longer, which was sad, because they'd had the very best start to it.

"Oh, Tyler, that's very generous. I'd best be going."

"It was certainly nice to see you." He let go of Courtney and she heard him walk to the door. Literally escorting her mother out.

When the door closed, Courtney sighed as she heard him walk back toward her. "She wears me out."

"She's out of sorts. Her son is gone and her daughter is moving on."

"Did you see how she belittled our event and my writing?"

He smoothed his hands over Courtney's hair and kissed her on the forehead. "And did you see how it all doesn't matter? You're here. I'm here. I made dinner. Let's eat."

CHAPTER 47

*T*he meal, Tyler thought, was fine. He was a good enough cook. But Courtney's mind was preoccupied—obviously still irritated with her mother.

This was new ground for him. As lost as he'd been over the truth about Darcy and what his mother had been through, he'd never really been irritated with his mother. Sure, annoyed when he'd gotten in trouble as a kid. Horrified when she'd caught him smoking with Jep out back when they were thirteen. Though that one made him want to laugh. The two of them had no idea what they were doing. But Jep had hijacked the cigarette from his dad and they were going to give it a try. Oh, was she ever mad.

But never had she blatantly discredited him as Mary had done to Courtney in the few minutes she was in Courtney's home. If that was how Courtney had grown up—and Fitz too—it was no wonder why Courtney wanted to fight to be independent. Being blind wasn't such a bad thing in contrast to living at home.

"I could certainly get used to you cooking like this," she said as she finished her bite and then sipped at her iced tea.

"I have about four meals I can cook well. This is one of them."

"Well, let's do this often." She laughed and reached for him.

"Thank you for handling her the way you did. I'm not sure I can convince you she's different, usually. This seems to be the only side you've seen."

"A woman with a very direct husband, a son who has been killed in combat, and a very independent daughter who doesn't need her all the time, is what I see. She's just a bit out of sorts."

"You always tell me I see more than sighted people. I can read them. But I think you do too."

"Sometimes when you're too close to it, you can't see what's going on."

"Like when you left."

He winced. "Exactly. I had to step away from it to realize my mom hadn't hurt me. She'd protected me by not telling me about everything. Spencer understood that. Me—I had to go have a pity party."

Courtney stood and moved to him, sitting down on his lap, and wrapping her arms around his neck. "I'm very glad your pity party ended when it did. I'm very happy that fate threw you on that plane."

"I'm just glad that when it did, I still smelled good."

She laughed and rested her head on his shoulder. "Let's clean this up and spend the rest of the night numbing our brain in front of the TV cuddled up."

"I think that sounds like a fine idea."

They moved in sync in the kitchen, cleaning dishes and wrapping up leftovers. Tyler washed the dishes and Courtney dried them. They laughed. They talked about the gala. They fell deeper in love over simple and everyday activities.

When everything was tidy and back in place—which was necessary for her safety and was going to take some work on Tyler's part—they moved toward the living room to spend their evening wrapped in each other's arms.

As they passed the table by the stairs, Tyler looked down at the basket filled with mail. "I've been meaning to ask you. Why do you have a basket of unopened mail?"

She stopped and turned to him. "I just put it there when it comes and my mother usually comes by and helps me take care of it. Mail doesn't usually come in braille. But I haven't been spending time with her. Oh, Tyler, there are probably some very important bills in there."

"Okay, let's take this into the kitchen and go through it. I'm here now. I can help you with this every day."

She nodded, but the crease between her brows told him that this was one of those cases where she needed someone's help and that bothered her.

Tyler picked up the basket and they walked back to the kitchen. For the next hour, they sorted envelopes according to what they were. Courtney pulled out her laptop and as Tyler told her what bill was to be paid. She entered it into the computer, and sent the payment through the bank.

Eventually the pile was dwindled down to junk mail, sale ads, and one letter.

"It's just addressed to the family of Fitz Field," he said.

"A sympathy card?"

"No, it must be a letter. No return address on it."

She lifted her hands in the air and sat back in her chair away from the computer. "Let's hear it then."

Tyler opened the letter and pulled out two sheets. One was crisp and pristine the other very obviously had been tattered and folded many times.

Tyler began to read, "To the family of Fitz. I hope I have waited long enough to send this letter. I was with Fitz when he was injured in combat. We had taken fire and he'd been hit in the leg. It wasn't a fatal wound, in fact, except for the chance of infection, it was only a flesh wound as the bullet hadn't even lodged itself in his leg." Tyler took a breath and continued.

"When we were able to take cover, we were in an area where

there was still heavy gunfire. We had the unfortunate moment to come across a young Afghan man who was very scared. He held us at gunpoint, but obviously he was in as wrong a place as we were.

"He shared with us his food and at one point Fitz asked him if he had something he could write on. Fitz spent the next few hours penning the note I have sent along.

"I know he was in some pain, but he'd not been himself in months. He was angry and spoke of his father many times. And on more than one occasion he mentioned that he never should have been in a war. He should have been home running some financial company. That was what he wanted to do. The military was never his choosing."

Tyler stopped for a moment and looked at Courtney whose face was pale. "Maybe we should stop for now."

"Are you kidding me?" she snapped out at him. "Finish the damn letter. In fact, read Fitz's letter. I want you to read Fitz's letter."

Tyler looked at the second piece of paper. It had been wet, ripped, and drenched in blood. But the only part of the letter he could read was the writing at the top.

"I can't read this. It's for you."

Courtney's lips pursed and her cheeks grew redder from anger mixed with the tears that were filling her eyes. "Don't mess around. I'm not kidding. Read it."

"The only part I can read says, For Courtney. Please get this to her." He swallowed and placed the letter in her hands. "It's in braille, done with the tip of a pen."

Her hands shook as she took the paper. "I taught him braille so we could send notes to each other and my mother would never be able to read them."

"I don't know how well you'll be able to read it. It has been folded."

Courtney set the paper flat on the table and gently skimmed

her fingers over the raised bumps on the paper. She did it repeatedly.

Her lips trembled. Her nose grew redder and she closed her eyes as the first tear rolled down her cheek.

"Can you read it? Do you understand it?"

She nodded and wiped her eyes.

"Sweetheart, what does it say?"

Courtney pulled the letter to her chest. "I think you need to go for now. I need some time alone."

"Courtney, what does it say?"

She stood from her chair, her hands flat on the table. "I said I need some time."

"And I want to know what's going on," he said as he rose.

Because he was fully aware that it was her house and she knew it like the back of her hand, there was no keeping up with her when she fled from him and ran up the stairs.

The door slammed and the lock clicked when he reached it.

"This is ridiculous. Why won't you tell me what he said?"

"I-want-to-be-alone," she screamed in almost a demonic voice.

Tyler stepped away from the door and went back to the kitchen where the other letter lay. He picked it up and finished from where he'd left off.

He began where the writer said; *The military was never his choosing.*

If I could call him a daredevil in combat, I would. He didn't show fear when standing down insurgents. But he did show great remorse if he took a life.

I highly believe that that and the lack of military desire, led to the following events.

We had promised to take turns sleeping. We were aware that we had been away from our squad for nearly going on two days. There was some chance we'd not be found. Though Fitz was sure they were near and would still come for us. During one of my sleeps, I was awaken by gunfire. When I rose I found our Afghan friend standing over Fitz's body holding a gun. He was shaken badly and was bleeding. I pulled my gun and began to interrogate him.

He said Fitz attacked him. But not in anger. He wanted the man to kill him. Fitz told him he wanted to die. When the man refused Fitz reached for the gun, and that was when it went off into his chest.

Tyler dropped the letter and sat down at the table. He ran his hand over his face and tried to breathe. Nausea bubbled in his stomach and he had to will it down. Fitz Field had committed suicide.

CHAPTER 48

*I*t had been nearly two weeks since Courtney had locked Tyler out of her room, out of the house, and out of her life.

He'd spent the night after finding out what was in the letter. He slept on the couch to be there when she needed him. The truth had been, she didn't need him.

Courtney had stood there the next morning and asked him to leave. No explanation. No apologies.

Tyler had done just that. Since then he'd called, texted, and stopped by. But for two weeks, he hadn't seen her or heard from her.

Perhaps she was mad because he'd called her father the next day. But Duane Field already knew about the letter and his daughter's reaction. He too was feeling the pain of his son's final words. However, with Courtney's wish in mind, he wouldn't agree to help Tyler see her.

"In time, and only when she's ready," he'd said on the front step of his home when Tyler had driven out.

"I understand. Please, sir, tell her I love her. I want to be there for her—for you all."

. . .

COURTNEY HEARD her mother sigh as she stepped back from the window. "He's gone," she said and Courtney nodded. "Don't you suppose you should talk to him? He seems to care a lot about you."

"He does. That's the problem."

"And how could that be a problem?" Her mother sat down next to her on the bed. "Don't you believe in the power of love?"

Courtney swallowed back the venomous anger she wanted to spew. Instead she took a deep breath and held it for a moment before letting it free.

"Mother, I can't be someone's burden ever again. I don't plan to be yours, and I certainly don't plan on giving this horrible life to someone else."

She heard the saddened tsk her mother made, but she didn't scold her. "What about the gala tomorrow? You've worked so hard. You should be there."

"No. I won't go. He can fire me, because I'm never doing that again."

Her mother patted her knee. "I'll be downstairs if you need me. Your father and I don't think you're a burden. And I don't think your brother thought you were either."

She felt her mother rise from the bed and heard the door close when her mother had left.

Courtney fell back onto the bed and sobbed again. How could Fitz have said such things in his letter? He resented their father for putting him into situations which had landed him where he was. *Who forces their son to train to kill others?* Fitz had written.

It still hurt—the sting of his words. Though he'd never said she was a burden, he'd apologized for the life he'd ended up giving her—a life of darkness and missed opportunities.

Who was he, the boy who'd taken his own life from them, to say she'd missed any opportunity? If he could have seen the life she painted in her mind, he'd never have done what he did. Fitz had been her life, and now he was gone by his own hand. It hurt. It hurt worse than having learned about it the first time. Worse than the day they collected his casket off the plane and her mother sobbed over it.

But Tyler had mended her heart and let her mourn her brother and accept his fate. How could she possibly accept this?

If Tyler ran when a blessing such as a sister arrived in his life, then he certainly would run from a woman who would always need and depend on him—or anyone for that matter.

It was better to let him grieve their brief affair and move on with his life. He'd be a foolish idiot if he didn't realize that his family was perfect. All of them. Even his mother who gave away her baby when it seemed darkest.

It stung to know that Tyler's family would accept her as she was forever. But then again, they wouldn't be the ones daily having to make sure everything was just right. Even children. Those children would come and she'd learn to adapt, but even their slight messes around the house could be dangerous. It was just better to say goodbye to the man and not think another thought of him.

Courtney sobbed until she no longer could tell light and dark. The sun had gone now, she knew. She was in her childhood bedroom—alone.

And she missed Tyler.

CHAPTER 49

*S*imone worked the room as she did so well. The event was bigger than Tyler could have ever imagined. There was a vendor that was supposed to be set up in the tents that was late. One of the sections of parking hadn't yet been opened. And of all people, Simone's father had shown up.

How come his arrival at the event hadn't shaken her up? After all, she'd barely spoken to her father in twenty years. Why show up now? Why here? Why bother?

However, Simone graced her guests with a smile and pure calm. So why did Courtney's absence make Tyler feel so off kilter?

"Honey, you did a wonderful job," his mother said as she approached him. "This is the best gala I think *Diamond Gift* has ever had."

"Thanks. I didn't do it alone though."

She smiled sweetly and reached out for his arm. "I know. Where is she?"

Tyler bit down hard so that he didn't snap back at his own mother when nothing was her fault. "I haven't seen her in two weeks. I've had to bury myself into final details here and, well, she hasn't been around."

Regan wasn't just any fool, and he knew that. And the way she scanned her eyes over him, he knew she was trying to pick up on what had happened. It was better to just tell her.

Tyler took a breath to give himself a moment. "She found out her brother wasn't killed in action, but he committed suicide."

His mother put her hand on her chest. "Oh, Tyler. That's horrible. You should go to her."

"I did, Mom. I've called, texted, emailed—no response. I go to her house, she won't answer. I go to her parents' house, and she won't see me. I'm lost."

The pain on his mother's face softened. "You love her."

He pulled out the ring he'd been carrying in his pocket for the past two weeks, showed it to her, and saw the first tear glisten in her eye.

"Before we got the letter from a man who knew what had happened, I'd asked her father for his blessing."

"And?" she asked with her eyes wide.

"He gave it to me." He looked down at the ring. "Avery helped me pick it out."

"When are you going to give it to her?"

Tyler dropped his shoulders and shoved the ring back into his pocket. "I was going to do it tonight. This was our project. It seemed fitting."

"You should give it to her tonight."

Was his mother not listening to him? She wasn't there. He hadn't spoken to her in weeks.

She stepped closer and rested her hands on his arms. "I love you. It hurt when you went away. It hurt more because I felt as though I pushed you away."

He took a breath to speak, but she shook her head.

"I've seen the two of you together. You're in love and that should get you through anything. She's hurting, Tyler. She's hurting in a way I hope you never know. Don't give up on her. Look," she said as she pointed toward Simone and her father dancing. "The strangest things can happen."

He nodded. "When this is over I'll head to her house again."

His mother kissed him on the cheek, caught sight of her granddaughter, and let out a little squeal. "I could use a house full of those," she said with a grin and hurried toward Darcy.

When Tyler moved toward the door to go check on events outside, he noticed Mr. and Mrs. Field walk in arm in arm.

His breath hitched. Was she with them? He didn't see her, but they'd seen him.

As they walked toward him, he felt the box in his pocket dig into his thigh. He swallowed hard and walked toward them trying hard to smile.

"Mr. Field." He held out his hand to shake the man's.

"Tyler." Duane Field looked around. "Quite impressive. You did a fine job here."

"Thank you, sir." He turned toward Mary Field and held out his hand. "Mrs. Field, it's nice to see you."

"Thank you for the invitation. We just had to see what our Courtney had been working on. I read the program, very impressive."

"The organization is very impressive. So is your daughter's writing. She did all the work on that herself."

He saw the flash of pride in her eyes.

Tyler steadied his breath. "How is Courtney?"

"Fine. Miserable. Lonely," her father said and didn't seem to have a bit of remorse when his wife elbowed him. "Mary, she's miserable. Why tell him a lie? She misses you like crazy and she's sucked up in a pity party."

"She loved Fitz very much," he offered.

"Yes she did. And he loved her too. But unfortunately the demons in his head got to him. And I regret the demons of war as well." He looked down at his wife's hand over his arm and gave it a pat.

Tyler knew the face of a man who carried regret. He'd looked at that face in the mirror for years.

"I'm honored that you came tonight. It means a lot."

Duane Field pushed his shoulders back and looked down at Tyler. "I might have told my wife about a little something you were planning. She wanted to see the ring."

Mary Field's eyes lit up. "That seems petty doesn't it?"

"No," he said pulling the ring from his pocket again and opening the box.

"Oh, Tyler that is stunning," she cried when she saw it. "She's going to love it."

"I'm not sure she will," Tyler said closing the box and sliding it back in his pocket. "I can't get her to talk to me."

"She's at her house," her father said. "I think that if you were to go to her, she might let you in."

"Really?" Tyler's voice rose in anticipation. "I love her," he said looking at both of them. "I want her to be my wife. I don't care that she's blind. I don't care that there will be many things that will have to be dealt with in our lives. I just want to be with her."

Duane Field nearly smiled. "I think she might be ready to hear that now." He looked at his wife. "Feel like dancing?"

She smiled. "I would love to."

The Fields walked away and spun into each other's arms with the music. I think she might be ready to hear that now—the words resonated in his ears.

"Who is that?" Darcy asked as she and Spencer walked toward him.

"Courtney's parents."

"I didn't see her here."

Tyler shook his head. "I haven't talked to her in weeks. She's not accepting the truth of her brother's death, now that she knows it. But," he looked toward her father, "he thinks maybe she'll let me in now."

Spencer placed his hand on Tyler's shoulder. "Go to her. We got this covered. Besides, if you don't give her that ring, it's going to wear a funny hole in your pocket." He smiled at him.

"How do you know about the ring? I really haven't told anyone."

"Avery picked it out," Darcy said on a laugh. "We all know."

What had he thought?

"I don't know what to do."

Darcy placed her hand on his cheek. "Together you will figure it out. Now go."

He hesitated for a moment then kissed his sister on the cheek and turned toward his brother.

"Dude, just get out of here," Spencer said taking a step back.

Tyler laughed with a nod. "I think I will."

CHAPTER 50

For a moment, Tyler sat in his car looking at Courtney's house. What if her parents were wrong? What if she didn't want to hear what he had to say now?

There was only one way to find out, and sitting in his car wasn't going to get him to where he wanted to be.

Tyler stepped out, shut the door, and walked up the steps to the house. If this didn't go well, could he live only a few blocks away from her and never think about her? Could he go on with his life in Nashville or would he need to relocate—again?

He knocked on the door and waited.

"Who is it?" Her voice was soft and sad on the other side of the door.

"Courtney, it's Tyler. Please let me in to talk to you."

It was quiet again. He waited for a moment, but it seemed like a lifetime, before he raised his hand to knock again. The door opened.

There she stood. Her hair was pulled up. Her clothes were well worn and comfortable. Her feet were bare, and her mother must have taken her for a pedicure to try and cheer her up, because her toes were bright pink.

In her arms she held the journal they had taken out of Fitz's room.

"Hi," he said in a weak attempt to win his way into the house.

"Why are you here? The gala is now. They need you."

"And I need you more."

She shook her head. "I'm not someone you can easily love. So you should go find someone who you won't have to burden yourself with the rest of your life."

"Are you kidding me? Is that what you think you are?" He stepped closer to the threshold without stepping over. "I'm sorry your brother died by his own hand. I'm sorry he scared the horse that made you see the world differently. But I'm not sorry you picked me up at the airport, and I'm not sorry I fell in love with you." He rested his hands on the doorjambs. "I don't want to lose you, and for the past few weeks I've been miserable. Please, just let me talk to you."

"If I let you in, will you leave when I ask you to?"

"Yes."

"Will you do me a favor while you're here?"

"Anything," he knew it sounded desperate.

She handed him the journal. "I need you to read this to me. I need to know what he was thinking."

Tyler took the journal and held it in his hands. "Okay."

Courtney stepped back into the house and walked toward the kitchen. Tyler followed, shutting the door behind him.

She was making tea and had already taken down a second cup by the time he'd walked into the kitchen. She hadn't offered him any, but she was making it.

Watching her, he realized just how much he'd missed her. He couldn't live without this woman in his life. So if she didn't accept his proposal he'd have to convince her in some way that they had to remain friends.

"Have a seat. I'll bring the tea to the table," she said.

Tyler sat quietly. He knew the process. She was thinking as

she took to the redundant task of making tea. When she was ready, she'd let him know.

Courtney eventually turned with both mugs of tea, walked to the table, and set them down.

"Thank you," Tyler said gratefully as she sat down at the table with him.

"I didn't even ask if you wanted it."

"I've missed having tea with you."

Courtney held her mug to her lips, blew, and then set it back down. "How is the gala?"

"Packed. Even Simone's father was there."

Her eyebrows lifted. "Really? Why?"

"I didn't ask. I was busy making sure everyone was where they were supposed to be."

Her head lowered. "I should have been there. I let everyone down."

It was a risk, but he reached across the table and rested his hand on hers. "You didn't let anyone down. You have things you need to deal with. Anyone who wouldn't understand that isn't human."

She picked up her mug again and took a sip of her tea. As she lowered it, she lifted her chin. "Do you have the journal?"

"I have it."

"Will you begin to read, please?"

He moved his chair closer to her and raised his hand to her cheek. "I will."

She placed her hand over his. "I don't know what to expect."

"You can expect that no matter what this book says, I'll be here when we're done reading it."

She nodded as he retracted his hand and opened the book.

The pages were filled with the handwriting of a man who influenced everything Tyler currently did, but whom he didn't know.

He started on the first page and read through years of a life cut so short. Fitz hated the military life, but he liked knowing his father was proud of him. Though he loved his mother, he couldn't stand to reside in her home, which was one of the reasons he'd bought the house Courtney lived in. He was happy that it had pissed his father off, but he was also happy to have Courtney out of her parents' house.

Court can do anything and everything on her own. Having the house gives her that opportunity. Under Mother's thumb she will forever be Mother's pet. And Dad needs to see her as something other than a disabled girl, she's anything but disabled.

Today I watched her saddle up a horse and take a long ride. I can't even imagine she'd want to be near a horse after what happened to her.

Tyler reached for her hand again and she took his, rubbing her thumb over his knuckles.

I know that if something had happened to me like that I wouldn't have been as strong as she always has been.

Tyler looked up at her and saw her lip tremble.

I know I was only four, but every day I feel horrible that she can't just hop into a car and drive away from everything. I can do that. She should be able to too.

I'm heading back for another deployment. I hate thinking I have to leave her, but I'm going to leave her the house. She deserves that.

I don't want to see more people die. I don't want to be the reason for their death. I can't live like this. I wish I had a little bit of the courage to go on as my sister does. She truly is my hero.

Tyler stopped as Courtney rested her face in her hands.

"Are you okay?"

She nodded. "I needed to hear that. I needed it so much."

Tyler moved toward her and gathered her into his arms. She wrapped hers around his neck and fell against him.

"You were his hero, not his burden,"Tyler confirmed.

"I miss him. I miss him so much."

"You should." Tyler eased her back and brushed her hair from her face. "I want to do something. Will you come with me?"

"Where are we going?"

"Let me just surprise you. Will you let me do that?"

The tension was visibly sliding away.

"Okay," she said smiling.

There might be hope for this after all, Tyler thought.

CHAPTER 51

*C*ourtney sat quietly in the car. Her brother loved her, she thought. But why couldn't she have been enough of a hero to him so that he'd come back to her?

The road beneath them changed. "Are we on a dirt road?"

"We sure are."

"Where are we going?"

He took her hand and laced their fingers together. "Two more miles and I'll tell you."

She nodded. Other than Fitz, she'd never trusted anyone as much as she trusted Tyler.

Five more minutes down the road, the car stopped.

"Okay, get out."

"Where are we?" she asked opening her door and setting her feet on the ground, getting a feel for the terrain.

She heard Tyler climb out of the car and walk around toward her.

"We're on the road leading up to my parents' house," he said taking her hands.

"Are we going for a walk?"

He chuckled. "No, c'mon." He led her around the heated hood

of the car. "We're going for a ride."

"So why did you stop?"

"Because you're going to drive us up to the house."

Courtney stopped. "Oh, no. You're crazy."

"No," he laughed. "I'm not crazy. C'mon, think of it as Fitz's wish for you. To drive away when it all gets too hard."

"Tyler…"

"Get in."

Her nerves fluttered in her chest, but she was actually giddy to try such a thing.

Tyler helped her into the car. "Okay, here's your seatbelt," he said handing it to her and she clicked it in. "I'm getting in and then I'll tell you everything."

She heard him on the gravel under his shoes and then heard him slide into the seat next to her.

"The car is in the middle of the road. There are a lot of trees, so we are going to take it very slow." He inched toward her. "Put your hand on the wheel." She followed his instruction. "With your right foot, feel for the pedals. On the left, the horizontal pedal is the brake."

"I have seen a car set-up, you know."

"Yeah, you're not eight. I'm still walking you through this."

Now she laughed. "Okay. I can feel the brake." She moved her foot over. "Now the gas."

"Right. Press down on the brake."

She did so, pushing it as far as she possibly could.

"Reach your right hand to your right." He guided her hand to the shift. "Keep your foot on that brake. Now, feel the button underneath?"

"Yeah."

"Press it in. Now click it down one and you're in reverse. One more click is neutral. One more click and you're in drive."

"I'm not really going to do this."

"Oh yes you are. Now put it in drive. Keep your foot on the

brake."

Courtney eased the shift down three clicks and she felt the car purr beneath her.

"Now, both hands on the wheel."

She gripped the wheel tightly and he laughed.

"Ease up a bit on the break."

Courtney shook her head. "I'm nervous. I might kill us both."

"Well, we'd be together."

"Tyler!"

He rested his hand on hers. "You're not even going to take your foot off the brake. But ease up just a bit."

Courtney let her foot ease up on the brake and the car began to roll. Quickly she pressed the pedal into the floor and the car jerked.

"Don't be afraid," he said, but the humor was heavy in his voice. "Ease up again."

Courtney let her foot ease up and the car began to roll again. "Oh, God!"

"Now just keep it where it is."

"Oh, Tyler. Don't let me crash."

"Keep going."

Courtney kept reminding herself to breathe. She could feel the road. The rise and fall of the ruts dug into the dirt.

"How fast are we going?"

She felt him move closer to her. "We haven't broken ten miles an hour."

Courtney laughed. "I can't believe you're letting me do this."

"You can do anything. Your brother said so."

Courtney bit down to keep her emotions tucked down. She hadn't thought she'd ever do this, but she was. She was driving away when everything seemed so hard.

"Turn your wheel the slightest bit to the right, there's a curve."

"I can't do this. Don't let me hit anything."

"You're not going to. Keep going."

She was driving. How was it possible? She'd always wanted to do this. When she was little, she'd sat on her father's lap and driven down private roads, just like she was doing right now.

Tyler gave her directions and she followed. A laugh burst through and Tyler's hand came to the wheel.

"Are you okay?" Now he was laughing too.

"Yes. This is amazing."

"Well, you've almost made it to the house."

She gripped the wheel tighter. "Don't let me hit anything."

"Just a little farther. We're almost to the house."

She pressed her foot down on the brake and the car jerked. "I can't go any farther."

"Put it in park."

Courtney reached for the shift and pushed it all the way to the top. Her hand shook when she let go of the gearshift and Tyler took it in his.

"You did it. You drove. You got in the car and drove."

"I did, didn't I?"

"Courtney, Fitz was right. There isn't anything you can't do."

She bit down on the inside of her cheek. There were tears coming and she wasn't sure she could stop them.

"Fitz loved you, but there was so much more going on in him. We can't even begin to understand what he saw. What he knew. But what we can do is live on knowing he loved you and carry on his spirit."

She nodded. "You're right. I still have to go on—even without him."

"But you have me," he said, raising his hand and caressing her cheek. "Hold on."

The door opened and Tyler stepped out. Courtney sat and waited for him. A moment later he opened the door. She turned toward him and swung her legs out and set her feet on the ground. Tyler took her hand and helped her from the car.

He offered his arm, but this time she laced her arm through

his and pulled him closer.

"Why are we at your parents' house?"

"Most private road I knew," he said on a laugh. "But there's more."

Tyler stopped walking. He turned her toward him and took her hands.

"When my mom ran from my dad, because of the circumstances surrounding her past, he didn't give up on her. He loved her more than what came before." He stepped closer to her. "I love you more than any burden you think you could be."

"Tyler, I love you. I never should have thought that's what I was."

"I'm happy to hear you say that. See, I had this amazing plan for tonight at the gala, but then you didn't show up."

"Oh, Tyler, I'm..."

He put his finger over her lips. "I want you to see something."

"See?" She smiled at him.

"The way you do. Here take a look."

He took her hand and turned it palm up. Then he set something in it. "What is it?"

"Look."

She let out a breath and wrapped her other hand around it. It was a velvet box, just like the one Fitz gave her with earrings.

Her hands began to tremble as she felt for the break between lid and bottom. She pushed open the top and stopped for a moment.

There was something about that instant you learned what the surprise was. She could use her lack of sight at her advantage for that moment. The box was open and she didn't know if it was a piece of candy, earrings, or—dear Lord—a ring.

"Aren't you going to touch it?" Tyler asked during her pause.

"I'm looking at it," she joked and he laughed.

Timidly she straightened her fingers and touched the item in the box. She bit down on her trembling lip when she felt the stone. He'd bought her a ring. A ring that would glisten in the sunlight, she could see. A ring that would be as silent on her finger as the dark she lived in. A ring that meant eternity—or so she assumed.

She raised her head. "Tyler…"

"It's beautiful, isn't it? It reminds me of you. Bright and shiny and simple and beautiful." He took the box from her hand. "Your father was happy it wasn't just a gold band. But you're not as plain as a gold band."

"My father?" She jerked back her shoulders. "You talked to him about this?"

Tyler moved in and rested his hand on her cheek. "Of course I did. A gentleman asks for a lady's hand in marriage. He doesn't just take it." He chuckled and she could almost feel his smile, because she knew he wore one.

"You're going to ask me to marry you?"

"I did that, remember? We agreed to wait until the time was right."

"And it's right?"

"It's right."

With her hand in his, she felt him move and the gravel crunched under his feet. He let out a few groans and snorted out a laugh. "Why is this part tradition? I just got a rock in my knee."

"You're proposing to me on one knee? Oh, God."

"Did you have something else in mind?"

She shook her head. "I didn't think anyone would ever propose to me ever. Go on."

Tyler cleared his throat. "From the very moment you dropped that scarf and I handed it back to you, I've been a little smitten with you. But with you by my side, even for a few hours, I was able to accept what had been dealt to me. I gained my life back when I met you and I gained a whole lot more. I fell in love, and I knew right away you were the one I wanted to share forever with."

The tears were rolling down her cheeks now. She lifted her free hand to her mouth to hold back the sobs, which would escape if she didn't.

Tyler gave her hand a squeeze. "Courtney, will you do me the honor of sharing forever with me? Will you marry me?"

Words didn't come so she nodded, hoping he'd notice. When she felt the ring slide onto her finger, she knew he'd seen her answer. A moment later, he was standing in front of her, pulling her in close with a kiss that could melt the stars from the sky.

"I love you, Courtney."

"Oh, Tyler, I love you too." She rested her head against his shoulder until she stopped crying. When she pulled back, she felt for the ring on her finger and gave it a good looking at. "This is beautiful. I can't believe you bought me such a beautiful ring."

"Avery helped. I'm not very good with picking out pretty things—except for my fiancée."

"I picked you out, remember?"

He laughed. "Right. I smelled good."

"You still do." She reached for his face and pressed a kiss to his lips. "So why did you bring me here to propose? I mean aside from the fact I blew off the gala?"

"This is where my father proposed to my mother. It seemed fitting, and that marriage has lasted a long time, and endured its share of things that would tear some apart."

"You're a very thoughtful man, Tyler Benson."

"I hope you always think so, because I will never be running away from anything again. Nothing can make me cower with you by my side. You taught me to accept the things I cannot change. And to face them head on with my chin high."

"I taught you that?"

"You did."

"Why don't we go home," she pulled him closer to her. "And I'll drive."

EPILOGUE

Courtney had wanted simple, and aside from the sheer size of Tyler's family, they'd managed to keep the guest list to a minimum. Now, seated among the women of her fiancé's family, in a guest room of Audrey Benson's home. Like many of Tyler's relatives before them, they would be married in Audrey's rose garden. Considering the longevity and sincerity of his own parent's marriage, he thought it would be good luck for them as well.

"Here, I have your tea," Clara took Courtney's hand and wrapped it around a mug. "Drink it before we put your dress on."

"I've been drinking tea for years without spilling it," she assured her.

"Yeah," Clara laughed, "but today your hands are shaking. Drink first."

Her hands were shaking, and there was no reason for it. One thing was for sure, she was embarking on the greatest day of her life, and there was no reason to be nervous.

The door to the room opened again and Courtney could smell her mother's perfume.

"Sweetheart, you're not dressed yet," her mother's voice grew near.

"I have time. I'm drinking my tea," Courtney said lifting her mug.

"Do you think I could have a moment alone?" her mother said softly, but Courtney knew just loud enough that her soon-to-be relatives heard.

Clara rested her hand on Courtney's arm. "We'll give you some time."

Courtney heard them all walk out of the room as her mother moved a chair to sit next to her.

Her mother took the tea from her and she heard her set it on the table. Then her mother took her hand and patted it.

"I'm going to be very honest," her mother began. "I never thought this day would come. And," she quickly added, "I probably hindered it for many years."

Courtney bit down on her lip to keep it from trembling.

Her mother turned Courtney's hand over and placed something in her palm.

"I want you to have this. Fitz gave it to me before he deployed the first time. It's a heart shaped locket, and inside is a photo of both of you. You were seven and he was three."

Courtney wrapped her hand around the locket and pressed it to her chest. "Thank you," she said softly, afraid her voice would crack with the tears that threatened.

"I'm so happy for you. I love Tyler. I love his entire family," her mother said taking her hand again. "You're going to be very happy, and I know he'll take good care of you. Well, you'll take care of one another. We know you don't need someone to take care of you."

Courtney leaned in and pulled her mother to her. The admission of her mother's acceptance of Courtney's independence was the only gift Courtney had ever wanted.

. . .

TYLER PACED in his the room that had been his grandfather's office.

"We've all been in your shoes," his father said as he poured all of the men in the room a shot of whiskey."

"Were you all as nervous as I am?" Tyler asked and every head bobbed in agreement.

Spencer laughed as he took his shot from their father. "I can't believe I'm the lone Keller man out there. And I am certainly in no hurry to get married."

Their uncle Carlos coughed out a laugh. "Good luck, kid," he aimed the jab at Spencer.

Tyler's father handed him his shot and placed his hand on Tyler's shoulder. "She's a catch, Ty. We've all been very lucky to find women who challenge us, and make us better men. Courtney is that woman. She belongs in this family."

COURTNEY STOOD in Audrey Benson's kitchen with her father. She was a moment away from full independence—and a lifetime with the man she loved.

"Are you ready?" her father patted her hand which held onto his arm.

"I am, Dad. I really am." She pressed her fingers to the locket, which she chose to wear with the locket open.

As the harpist began to play, her father kissed her on the cheek. "I'm proud to have you as my daughter," he said, and Courtney wondered why everyone said beautiful things that threatened to make her cry.

TYLER WATCHED as Courtney and her father walked toward him. Spencer leaned closer to him. "She's beautiful."

What could Tyler say to that? He'd never seen a woman more radiant.

When they had reached him, her father stopped, kissed Courtney on the cheek, and then held his hand out to Tyler.

"I know she's in good hands with you, son."

"She is, sir," Tyler promised.

"And I know you're in good hands, too. She'll take good care of you," her father said smiling before he moved to sit with Courtney's mother, who was already crying.

"You look amazing," Tyler said as he took Courtney's hands.

"And you smell good."

"That's a good sign." Tyler lifted the locket on her neck and looked at it. "This is new."

"Fitz gave it to my mother. She gave it to me."

"And you're wearing it open so he can be here?"

Courtney nodded. "Without him, I wouldn't believe in myself enough to pick up men on airplanes. And without him, I wouldn't have been on that airplane. With him looking on, I can show him how amazing the world is that I see."

Tyler cupped her face in his hands. "I love you, Courtney. I promise you a lifetime of love, no matter what life throws at us."

"I know. I don't need to see your face to know that you smile when you say you love me. I can hear it."

Tyler leaned in and kissed her. "Let's make this official. I can't wait another moment to start this amazing life, and to see it the way that you do."

We hope you enjoyed Bernadette Marie's *The Acceptance*.
Continue the family saga with an excerpt from book two, *Merger*.

INTERNATIONAL BESTSELLING AUTHOR

BERNADETTE MARIE

THE MERGER

THE KELLER FAMILY SERIES
BOOK NINE

BESTSELLING AUTHOR OF
THE THREE MRS. MONROES TRILOGY

THE MERGER

CHAPTER ONE

*O*regon was a fine place. Perhaps, Spencer Benson thought, he'd like to come back someday and visit as a tourist. However he was into his fifth month of merger negotiations with Pacific Line Lumber, and his desire to ever fly out to the Pacific coast again was waning.

He pressed his head to the back of the boardroom chair as he listened to the eighty-year-old owner of the company reminisce, again, about the day his father had taken down the first tree to build their family house—and an empire was born.

Spencer had a great appreciation for family business. He was part of one. His great-grandfather had started Benson, Benson, and Hart. His grandfather took over, followed by his father. His cousin Ed had been holding the CEO position for years now. It was time for him to rise to the position. However, taking five months to close a deal wasn't making him shine.

A moment later, the door opened, and Spencer felt the twinge in his chest start as it did every time that bitch of a lawyer walked in the door. Julie Jacobson had found a million little flaws in the proposal. He'd like to not see her face again.

Okay, he thought, it wasn't a bad face. She wore her blonde

hair back in a ponytail most times. Her eyes were brown. He'd noticed that as she'd burned holes through him for the past five months with them.

Today she hurried into the boardroom dropping a stack of paper on the table. It toppled over, slid to the floor, and she scrambled to pick it up as every man in the room watched.

Okay, he'd later admit he'd rather have watched her fume over the papers and thought it was just, but he wasn't that kind of man. Spencer rose from his seat and walked across the room to help the frazzled lawyer with the mess she'd created.

When everything was stacked back on the table, she turned those brown eyes on him. They were bloodshot and full of sadness.

"Thank you," she said very softly as if not to let the rest of the room hear her.

"My pleasure," he lied and walked back to his seat.

The meeting continued with interludes from the owner as he reminisced about this or that. A brief five hours later, they finally broke and Spencer gathered his things and headed back to his hotel.

As he walked through the lobby, his phone rang. It was his father and he toyed with the idea of not answering it. However, that wasn't like him either.

"Hey, Dad."

"Make any progress?"

Spencer blew out a breath. "You know that lawyer is making me crazy. We're up to replanting. How many trees and seedlings will we replant each year to replace everything we use. We've gone over that."

His father laughed. "And how many will we?"

"I don't know," he said pushing the button to the elevator. "I have a lot of math to do tonight."

"This is your project. You'll do fine with it."

"Sure, you just don't get what a piece of work this woman is," he said just as he noticed that very woman step into the elevator as the doors closed. He let out a grunt. "Dad, I'll talk to you later."

He disconnected the call and shoved his phone back into his pocket.

Julie Jacobson didn't turn to look at him. She didn't say a word to him. But there was something going on inside of her. Something was wrong. Why was she in the hotel elevator?

Was she crying?

Oh, who cared? She deserved to cry. She was costing him time and money each time she opened her damn mouth in that board-room, and he was tired of her. Let her cry.

The elevator opened again and another man walked in, looked her up and down, then he pushed a button. The elevator rose a mere two floors before the man got off. Spencer watched as Julie literally stomped her foot in aggravation for the stop.

They rode in silence for a few more floors, and then the doors opened. Spencer began to step off, but the blood that ran through him wouldn't let a woman suffer. He lodged his hand in the door and looked at her. She was indeed crying.

"Ms. Jacobson, are you okay?"

She lifted her head. The woman with the attitude didn't seem to be looking back at him. This was a broken woman with troubles. He could see that. She only nodded and he accepted her answer.

"Okay, then, have a pleasant night." He stepped back again, but when her head lifted again, and the sadness burned through him, he couldn't handle it. He tucked his foot back into the door forcing it open.

"Mr. Benson, what are you doing? I'd like to get to my room, please."

Ah, there she was, he thought as he stepped back into the elevator and the door closed behind him.

"You don't look okay. I mean something's going on and I just want to be here if you need someone."

She let out a grunt. "You hate me. I know you hate me. I'm costing you time and money." So, she was a mind reader. "My private life, on the other hand, isn't any of your business."

He nodded. He could accept that.

She lifted her hands to wipe away the tears and he noticed the sign of a wedding ring having recently been taken off. There was an indent in her finger, and a white line where it must have been worn for years.

"Would you be interested in having a drink?"

She turned to him and those brown eyes bore right through him. "Are you kidding me? You want to take me out for a drink? I'm the lawyer for the company you're trying to buy. I don't think that would look very good, do you?"

He hadn't thought of that. "No. You're right. I just..."

He only had a moment to catch his breath before the woman lunged at him and pushed him up against the wall of the elevator. Spencer was ready for the knee to the groin, but her mouth coming down on his, her tongue pressing into his mouth, her hands in his hair—none of that he'd expected.

Spencer was gripping the bar on the wall, but the man in him decided that a woman throwing herself at him would be better to hold. He placed his hands on her hips and pulled her to him even tighter. Heat rose between them. The moan from her throat was enough to make him go light headed as the blood traveled away from his brain.

When the door opened, Julie stood straight and stepped away from him. As Spencer moved to her, she held up her hand and straightened her shoulders.

Her breath was coming in great big gasps. Pink colored her cheeks and those brown eyes didn't hold fire.

"Good night, Mr. Benson," she said as she stepped out of the elevator.

Goodnight? What in the hell? His body wasn't quick enough

to chase after her before the doors closed and she was out of his sight.

The blood was rushing back to his head and he thought he might need a very cold shower when he got back to his room.

What was that all about? Bitch one moment—panting horny woman the next?

Who needed it? This was just the force and fire he needed to walk into that meeting tomorrow and say take it or leave it. He'd had enough of Pacific Line Lumber and their legal staff.

He pushed the button for his floor.

As the door opened, Spencer stepped out onto his floor and went straight to his room. He slid the keycard into the lock, and then again, and again. He hated these stupid pieces of plastic. Finally, the door beeped and he pushed it open.

The lightness in his head took over. He was going to need to sit down.

He knew this feeling. He'd had it before. Crap! That woman had kissed him senseless. That's what it was.

Something was up with the blonde with those dark, burning eyes. Never before would he have imagined a woman like her in tears. No, something was hurting her—or someone. He'd make sure to take the time tomorrow and find out what was going on.

Spencer sat down on his bed and lay back. He closed his eyes. The heat of that kiss swam in his head again. Her hips under his hands. Her body pressed to his.

Oh, hell, she'd messed with his mind.

Tomorrow, she'd finally see his fire. She wasn't going to mess with him like this. All hell was going to break loose tomorrow.

For now, though, he was going to take a very long, very cold shower.

ABOUT THE AUTHOR

Bestselling Author Bernadette Marie is known for building families readers want to be part of. Her series The Keller Family has graced bestseller charts since its release in 2011. Since then she has authored and published over fifty books. The married mother of five sons promises romances with a Happily Ever After always...and says she can write it because she lives it.

Obsessed with the art of writing and the business of publishing, chronic entrepreneur Bernadette Marie established her own publishing house, 5 Prince Publishing, in 2011 to bring her own work to market as well as offer an opportunity for fresh voices in fiction to find a home as well.

When not immersed in the writing/publishing world, Bernadette Marie can be found spending time with her family, traveling (mostly to Disney parks), and running multiple businesses. An avid martial artist, Bernadette Marie is a second degree black belt in Tang Soo Do, and loves Tai Chi. She is a retired hockey mom, a lover of a good stout craft beer, and might have an unhealthy addiction to chocolate.